The Remembering

The Remembering

Dione Orrom

Troubador Publishing Ltd
Unit E2 Airfield Business Park,
Harrison Road, Market Harborough,
Leicestershire LE16 7UL
Tel: 0116 279 2299
Email: books@troubador.co.uk
Web: www.troubador.co.uk

ISBN 978-1-80514-357-4

British Library Cataloguing in Publication Data.
A catalogue record for this book is available from the British Library.

Printed and bound in Great Britain by 4edge Limited
Typeset in 11pt Minion Pro by Troubador Publishing Ltd, Leicester, UK

For our beautiful planet and wonderous natural world.
For Obi, who led our woodland adventures,
and of course, Nick, Sula, Cal and Lucy.

The information about the trees and plants contained in this book are based on established folklore and herbal information; however, this is a work of fiction – please do not eat wild plants or their fruits without checking with a knowledgeable adult or learning from an expert. If you are interested, there are lots of books and information online on edible plants and trees.

"Since the dawn of time, a being has lived deep in the earth. It is said it came from the stars and settled in the earth's core, undisturbed. It acted as a kind of pendulum, holding the balance in the darkness. But, when the destruction started, the being fed on the sadness that came with it; it did this in an attempt to rid the world of it, but the balance faltered and, with time, it has become the sadness, the destruction, become the nothingness. It carries a numbing, as if it wants to suck everything back into the void and the ancient shadows. The balance lost. We call it The Forgetting."

Taxus the Yew.

Chapter 1

"*You will be OK, Jack, don't forget the trees*," his dad's voice echoed in his head.

Jack buried his face in Stan's warm fur, breathing in the familiar musty, sweet smell of his dog, trying to shut out the day. He closed his eyes and thumped the bed hard with his fist. Stan wriggled out from under him, got off the bed, clawed open the door and disappeared down the stairs. Jack rolled onto his back and stared up at the old yellow stars they had stuck on the ceiling when he was little. All those nights he had sat under those stars, listening to his dad's stories about the woods, right now, he wanted to peel them off and throw them away, but they were way out of reach. He sat up and looked out of the window at the oak tree in Tom and Mia's garden next door, its spring leaves bright in the morning sun.

Turning away, he pulled on a pair of jeans, T-shirt and a hoody. He picked up a small carved wolf that sat on his desk, rolling it around in his fingers, remembering his dad whittling it out of a broken beech branch. It was simple with rough edges, but he loved it. Pushing it into his pocket, he tramped down to the kitchen, head down, hoping to avoid eye contact with his mum. He felt encased in a repelling magnetic field, he just wanted to get outside, away from everyone.

"Is it OK if I take Stan to the woods?" he muttered, grabbing Stan's lead.

"Really?"

"Please, Mum."

"OK, but phone, Jack!" said his mum, thrusting his mobile into his hand. "Please turn it on! I need to know where you are."

He could tell she was trying not to sound too pushy.

"OK, sorry," he mumbled.

He shoved the phone in his pocket and headed out; Stan obediently stayed at his heels and kept looking up at him with his soft, brown eyes. He put his hand down and touched his dog's warm, scruffy head. It had been his dad's suggestion he get a puppy, his very own 'wolf'. Jack remembered the first time he held Stan as a tiny pup in his arms: those eyes looking up at him, his strange, musky smell and how the nurses had allowed him to sneak Stan into the hospital to show his dad. He looked at Stan, who was watching him quietly – he had been there through it all. He scrunched up his eyes to stop the stinging, shaking his head as if to rid himself of the thought, and set off down the lane.

As he reached the line of small shops, he shoved his hands in his pockets and started walking fast. There was a shout from across the street. Looking up, he saw Mia and Tom standing with a bunch of people, their demon pack. They were all staring in his direction; he hadn't even thought about it being a school day. His heart started racing. *Not today, just not today,* he thought, and started to run. He ran past the shops, dodged pushchairs and children; sharp shouts of 'careful', 'slow down' followed him. He ran on, past the church, past the turning to school, scrambled over the five-bar gate and on up the hill; he didn't stop until he got to the edge of the wood. His breath rasping, tears and sweat making streaky lines down his face, he held Stan, digging his fingers into his dog's warm fur, scouring the hill below. A smog-like haze hung over the small town, and in the distance, cars were zipping along the bypass in the valley, but nothing moved. Had they followed? Would they skip school just to harass him? He knew they would be tempted, but woods were out of their comfort zone. Woods 'whispered' of mystery and dark unknowns, and old tales still lingered about these woods being haunted by a strange old woman, but for him, woods were about building dens and playing for hours with his dad and their beloved trees. He started to relax a little, then something caught his eye – was someone moving below him? Without a second thought, he turned and darted into the wood, stumbling over tree roots and the thick ivy that curled across the ground, Stan bounding at his heels.

Breathless, he stopped by a huge, ancient beech tree. He put his hand out for support, touching the familiar grey-green bark, trying to calm his thoughts; a tingle ran down his spine. The tree's huge roots spread under his feet; on one side of the tree was a large, inviting hollow. He sat down, pushing himself into the recess, just wanting everything to be different. Stan nuzzled in at his side. His mind spun with all the teasing, the taunts outside class. He had thought they would be friends, Mia and Tom, the twins – they were his neighbours after all – but instead they had chosen him to humiliate, and now even home didn't feel safe. He sat, enveloped by the tree, wishing he was with his dad, listening to his stories about the trees. He looked up at the bright-green leaves of the canopy, turning the wolf carving in his fingers. Suddenly, a hard jolt tugged his belly, his body jerked, then he felt as if he was sliding downwards, being thrown from side to side in some kind of tunnel, twisting through the earth. He squinted through his half-closed eyes: shapes moved past him, huge roots, tiny filaments, tails of worms, legs of beetles, flashes of holes heading off somewhere into the darkness. Something wet thwacked him in the face, and a loud pulsing sound vibrated through him, like chainsaw cutting through wood. His whole body tensed; he squeezed his eyes up tight, but his mind was suddenly flooded with images: Tom's intimidating face right up close, laughing; harsh 'blinking' messages on his phone screen; a coffin disappearing behind a velvet curtain. He screamed. His body lurched, like he was being pulled to a sudden stop, and he fell sideways with a thud.

Chapter 2

Jack lay for a moment, his breathing tight. He gulped some short breaths. His eyes felt glued together; he hardly dared open them. His heart was pounding in his ears, but around him was silence – there was none of the usual far-off traffic noise, no overhead planes and no chainsaws or weird pulsing sounds. Slowly, he forced open his eyes, just enough to peer through his eyelashes. Looming over him was the same enormous, grey-green beech tree trunk. He pressed his fingers into the old, rotting leaves beside him, a familiar rich earthy smell filled his nose, relaxing him, just a little. Opening his eyes fully, he pushed himself up to sitting. Holding Stan tight with one hand, his wolf carving pressed into the palm of the other, he gazed around, realising that both he and the tree seemed to be in a different place.

"What happened?" he muttered into Stan's fur. "I'm scared."

Stan was sniffing the air intently. Jack followed his

dog's gaze and saw that the beech tree was part of a circle of magnificent ancient trees – they were majestic, with huge, broad trunks and branches reaching up to the sky above. The clearing at the centre was filled with light, and the bright-green spring leaves made shadows dance across the glade. Everything felt familiar but different. His heart was still thumping hard; he lay his face on his dog's neck and tried to calm his breathing.

"Stan, where are we?" he murmured, fear and awe mingled in his voice.

Stan nuzzled him.

"I guess we need to take a look." Jack's whisper was tentative.

Slowly, curiously, he started to look around. He ran his fingers along the ancient trees' bark; they were mesmerising. There were scratches on the trunk of a huge birch tree – his mind swirled, *an antler, or claws?* He gingerly reached up to touch the tendril-like creepers hanging from the branches of a gnarled old hawthorn tree, a shiver ran down his spine, he snatched his hand back, half expecting them to grab his hand. He laughed a little at himself.

"Stan, what has happened? Where are we?"

An abrupt, loud cracking noise made him jump; he spun around, grabbing Stan, staring into the dark of the trees around him. *What was that?* A blast of a cold wind suddenly blew across his face, a sharp, acrid smell filled his nostrils, a smell like burning plastic, clawing and unpleasant. Then, suddenly, from out of the darkness, people burst out of the trees with shouts of, "It's coming, it's coming." They were all running at speed towards something the other side of the glade; Jack couldn't see what they were heading for.

"What is it?" He gasped. "Hello! Help!" he called.

No one stopped; no one answered – they all seemed too focused on getting somewhere he couldn't see. In sheer confusion, he started to run, not knowing where he was running to or why, but he could hear feet pounding up behind him. He started to run faster, when a hand grabbed him and pulled him forcefully.

"Jack, quickly," a girl's voice shouted, "you must come with me *now*!"

He tried to pull away, but the girl held on tight, jerking his arm; she was strong. How did she know his name? He faltered for a split second, just long enough to allow her to yank him along behind her. He saw a flash of grey fur out of the corner of his eye.

"Stan!" he yelled.

Before he could pull away, the girl dragged him into a huge hollow inside a massive old yew tree, on the edge of the glade, just as fat drops of rain started to hit the ground.

"Stan!" he screamed again.

Stan darted in through people's legs and pushed himself onto Jack's feet.

Jack stood rooted, his legs heavy, gasping for breath. There were so many people squashed into the giant hollow of the tree; it was uncomfortable and awkward. They were all holding on to each other, muttering in fear. Like the girl, they were dressed in rough-looking muted brown and green clothes. Jack tried to shrink himself away, but there was no room to move.

"Where am I?" he stammered.

"I am so sorry, Jack; you were not meant to meet us this way. It is *a Breaking*," the girl said hurriedly.

He stared at her, speechless. She was a bit older than him, he guessed. Sweat was sticking her curly dark hair to her forehead.

"I'm Aster," she said, smiling.

"What exactly is happening? And how do you know my name?"

"I am sorry, Jack, there is so much to tell you," said Aster, looking him straight in the eye. He was almost shocked by the kindness in her eyes.

"And what do you mean by 'a breaking'?"

"A Breaking is when The Forgetting splits out, from deep in the earth, and becomes what we call Dark Rain."

"Right, that makes sense," he mumbled, looking out at the giant drips sliding slowly down the trees, but as he watched, he realised something didn't look normal – the drips seemed to be thick and gooey, like slime.

"Jack, we need you to help us," said Aster.

"What?" said Jack.

"Please, do not be afraid, Jack." A different voice reverberated around them.

It was a gentle but strong voice, and strangely reminded Jack of his grandma. He looked up and around him. No one else seemed to respond.

"Who is that?"

"I am Taxus the Yew," came the echoing voice from above. "I am a Tree Elder, and member of the Tree Council, I have lived on this earth for four thousand sun years – I have seen a lot. This is not quite how we planned to meet you, but we are so very glad you are here."

"Where exactly *is* here?" Jack whispered with a slight stammer.

"Don't be afraid," said Taxus.

"Right, yeah," muttered Jack.

Jack was hot and squashed inside the tree, his T-shirt stuck to his sweaty back. He wriggled his fingers deep into Stan's reassuring fur.

"Jack, you are in the ancient forest which used to cover the land where your town is. In your time, all that is left is the wood on the hill where you used to play with your dad, where you came to this morning. The Tree Elders have watched you for some years and have waited for so long to really meet you. Your visit to us today is most precious and so welcome," said Taxus gently.

"What? But how did I get here?" he asked, his tummy fluttering.

"We brought you here through our ancient Root Network, woven by the trees and fungi through the Rings of Time – it connects all things."

"The Root Network," Jack muttered almost to himself, mulling the words over. "And you brought me here?" he repeated. "Of course, right."

"It is a web, Jack, like your blood vessels, or the

synapses of a brain. It is very powerful and is of utmost importance to us all," said Taxus slowly.

Staring out of the hollow, Jack realised that the giant yew was part of the circle of trees surrounding the glade; their intricate roots laced the floor. The weird rain was stopping; the last heavy drips slid off the leaves, landing with a rhythmical *thud, thud*, leaving shiny, slug-like trails down the old, gnarled trunks.

"Jack, we know it will sound crazy to you, but we need to tell you something that is most important."

At that moment, there was a sudden gasp from the people around him. Outside, the strange raindrops were forming into mercury-like silvery puddles, slithering along the ground towards Taxus; it was as if they were alive. There was a loud rattle from the branches of the trees in the circle around them, and their roots started glowing with a gold light. Abruptly, the strange, silver puddles recoiled with a hiss and shrunk away, repelled by something, slinking into a crack in the ground.

"What *was* that?" asked Jack.

"That," came the calm voice of Taxus the Yew, "was a liquid sadness, a numbing, it is seeping through from your time. We call it The Forgetting. Our Root Network held it back for now; The Forgetting is not yet strong enough to cross our web."

"Forgetting, what?" asked Jack. Nothing was making sense now.

"There is a lot to explain," said Aster. "We *need* you, Jack."

The people around him seemed to relax and were slowly venturing out from inside the tree.

"Come," said Aster.

"You must meet the rest of the Tree Council," said Taxus.

"What?"

A rustle in the branches rippled around the glade.

"Jack, welcome. Please do not be afraid; we know this is all very strange for you," came a new, deep voice. "I am Ogham the Oak, Leader of the Tree Council."

The voice, Jack realised, was coming from the huge, crooked oak tree in front of him; the branches rustled a little as it spoke.

"You know me, Jack, you have sat by me often with your dad in the wood."

Jack reached up and ran his fingers down the deep-grooved bark of the tree; his fingers tingled. He looked up at its massive, outstretched, arm-like branches. How could it be the same tree?

"The other tree you have met today, the tree you sat with, is Feya the Beech, Gatekeeper to The Tree Council. Beech trees carry the old wisdom, and her ancient powers meant she could bring you to our council circle. It should have been a very special moment, but then the Breaking confused everything, for that I am sorry." Ogham spoke clearly; his voice had a slight echo to it which reverberated through the wood after he spoke.

"Hello, Jack," came the soft, singing tones of Feya the Beech. "I am so glad you are here," she said, her leaves dancing above him. "Please put your hand on my bark. I can help you to understand things that maybe your mind will struggle to comprehend."

Jack turned and tentatively reached out his hand and rubbed it down the beech tree's smooth bark; he had always loved the soft, grey tones of beech trunks – they were so familiar to him. Memories flooded back: sitting with his dad, watching the squirrels collecting the nuts for winter and making little characters our of beechnut shells. His breathing calmed.

"Around the circle are the mighty ancient trees of birch, alder, hawthorn, lime, hornbeam and ash," said Ogham.

The other trees called 'hello' in unison, their leaves moving gently as if waving.

"We are the Tree Council; we are Tree Elders, and that gives us special powers," said Ogham, his deep voice soothing and kind.

"How come I can hear you?" asked Jack.

"Here, the old powers still exist, which means you can hear us. We have been observing you, Jack, since you were very young and came to the woods with your dad. We thought we might have lost you when your dad was ill, but today, something very special has occurred to allow us to meet. We are so sorry, Jack, that your father died, so, so sorry. He was a special person, and he gave us such hope. We are here for you now."

Jack looked up in an attempt to stop the jolt of sadness that hit him. He stared at the trunk of the mighty tree; a pair of round eyes met his, as a little owl peered from a hole in the trunk and slowly blinked its deep, inquisitive eyes. Jack blinked back. The echo of his dad's voice rang in his head again, "*Don't forget the trees Jack.*"

"Jack, we are running out of time," said Ogham. "We need someone to help us, someone who knows, who understands."

"Understands what? How do you know about my dad?" Jack's voice wobbled with confusion. "I don't understand anything, *and* the beech tree where I sat down was somewhere different," Jack protested quietly.

"Things are sometimes a little changeable around here, as you will discover. It is not quite as straightforward as you may think," continued Ogham. "As Elders, we have lived longer than you will believe is possible, awarding us immense knowledge and freedom. When a Tree Elder dies, their spirit travels through the root and fungi system, the Root Network, to another young sapling, and that way, our knowledge can be protected and maintained. We can move to different tree forms, and to different times, which means things are not quite as fixed as you might believe or have been taught," said Ogham.

"But I thought those were just my dad's stories." Jack's voice was a mix of enthusiasm and scepticism. "It is not real."

"Jack, your dad was a great friend to the Elders. He was a special man and one of the few remaining who still knew how to speak with us," interjected Ogham gently. "He wanted you to learn too; that's why he brought you to the woods, to us." Ogham's tone was kind and tender. "You can hear us now."

Jack wanted to believe, remembering how he thought he heard trees talk when he was little, but old taunts were pushing into his mind. "*Hey, Flakey, have you been talking to the plants?*" His stomach knotted. He looked down at Stan, who was gazing up at him, grinning his toothy grin. Stan nudged him with his wet nose. He couldn't help smiling at his scraggy-haired dog.

"Through the Root Network, Jack, we can communicate across the world, with the Tree Elders and councils from other lands: the powerful sequoias and bristlecone pines of California, the banyan and peepal in India, the huge kapok trees of the rainforests – the ones who still stand, that is – and the mighty Pando, the aspens of Utah. In your time, we are hearing the same story over and over again, whisperings of the world faltering, losing its balance. We have little time left and need to act quickly," said Ogham.

"We are so glad you made it to us. A person from your time is the last piece of the puzzle and the only hope we have." The strong voice of Taxus rang out across the glade.

"There is much to show you. Your father did so want to help the trees. It is tragic that he could not. We need you. Will you trust us, Jack?" asked Ogham.

A sudden shriek stopped him mid-sentence. Jack recoiled and Stan stood alert, sniffing the air. Everyone went silent. A girl came cowering out of the trees; the silvery, slimy 'rain' clung to her clothes and hair. There was a sharp gasp from Aster. The girl stood out in the open, her face drained of colour, her sobs reverberating through the trees. A woman the other side of the glade, recognising her daughter, wailed, but stood stock still, her instinct to go to her overpowered by the fear of touching her. For a moment, no one moved; everyone was silent. Then an older woman stepped forward from in the trees, walked over to the girl and silently gestured for her to take off her 'wet' and sticky overgarments. She wrapped her in her shawl and carried her out of the glade, the mother walking silently behind. Aster turned and ran after them. Jack stood alone in the circle of the trees.

"What happened?" asked Jack.

"She has been touched by the Dark Rain and will be tainted by The Forgetting. This is what we need to tell you, and why you are here," said Taxus, her voice deep and wise.

Jack stared into the wood, to the darkness where the girl and Aster had gone. He stood quiet and alone for some time, trying to make sense of everything, his mind tumbling and reliving what had just happened. Something about the trees did feel familiar.

"Jack," echoed the gentle voice of Taxus. "What you must understand is that once, all beings, plants, animals and humans communicated with each other, like we are now. The trees and plants shared with the humans and animals what could be eaten, and what from our branches, roots and fruit was good for healing and medicine. Humans only ever took from us what was absolutely necessary. The knowledge was carried through the Root

Network, and there was a balance in the earth." Taxus paused for a moment.

Jack tried to grasp what the old tree was saying: his dad's stories were true – people once really had been able to hear trees, plants and animals. He gazed out at the wood.

"Then, Jack, things started to change," said Taxus. "People started taking from the natural world more than they needed; they took from us for profit, for greed, and a terrible cycle was started. They started losing the ability to hear us and became more and more separate, and the more separate, the more they destroyed, and the more they destroyed, the more they forgot," said Taxus, her voice serious and passionate. "They forgot about the balance of the world."

"But I really don't understand. What was that weird rain, and what happened to the girl?" said Jack quietly.

"Since the dawn of time, a being has lived deep in the earth. It is said it came from the stars and settled in the earth's core, undisturbed. It acted as a kind of pendulum, holding the balance in the darkness. But, when the destruction started, the being fed on the sadness that came with it; it did this in an attempt to rid the world of it, but the balance faltered and, with time, it has become the sadness, the destruction, become the nothingness. It carries a numbing, as if it wants to suck everything back into the void and the ancient shadows. The balance lost." Taxus paused for a moment, as if the words were thick in her mouth and hard to say. "We call it The Forgetting."

The words burned inside Jack, like he could feel the pain of that being. Agitatedly, he scratched the back of his hand; his skin stung. Stan gently nuzzled his hand away.

"But what has that got to do with this Dark Rain and my dad and *me* being here?"

"We need you, Jack," said Taxus slowly. "As The Forgetting grows, the balance goes and so the Root Network is starting to break down. The sad force is seeping into our world in different ways, and one of those ways is Dark Rain. If the Dark Rain touches people, they too forget and turn away from nature. But the rain is only part of it – when its force is too great, it will push through and cause ultimate destruction."

"Where did it go just now?" asked Jack.

"It returned to the deep earth. But the stronger it becomes, the weaker we and the Root Network become. We will not be able to hold it back for long."

"And then what?"

"That is what we need to explain, why we need you," said Taxus.

"In your time, only very few people have kept the ability to listen, to hear us. Just some isolated cultures, those who know the ancient laws and the likes of your dad and you, Jack. Lone voices," said Taxus. "We need your help."

"There's a lot to tell you, Jack," said a strange, friendly voice from somewhere near his feet.

"What!" Jack shrieked, looking down at his feet. Was he mad?

Stan started barking and bouncing around, like he used to do when he was a puppy.

"Jack, Jack, Jack," he barked.

"Stan?!" said Jack, laughing in total disbelief. "I can hear you!"

"Like Taxus says, this is how it was once."

"It shows us there is hope, Jack," said Taxus joyfully.

"Stan, how come you have never spoken before?"

"We were in a different time, and you were not ready – my tail had to do the talking!"

"I am not sure I can get my head around this!" said Jack, his mind flipping out. "So, you have understood everything I have said to you?"

"Well, maybe not everything!" said Stan.

"And my dad really met the Tree Council?"

"He did. You remember how he would tell you stories all about the trees and what to look for. He had always talked about trees like they were friends because they were!" Stan licked Jack's hands. Jack sat down, hugging his dog hard.

"There is a lot to tell you about pets," said Stan.

Jack laughed. "Oh, what is that?"

"Well, some animal friends chose a path to try and help the humans to remember. They gave themselves in service to man and to 'the human cause'. Certain species have aligned themselves closely with humans to keep them in some way connected to the natural world around them."

"What do you mean?" asked Jack.

"Pets, Jack. Pets are animals that have been in service to man, to try and help. Dogs have, of course, led the way!" said Stan, laughing a little as he put his head on one side.

Jack started to laugh. Stan's tail didn't stop wagging.

"It is true, you know, seriously. Having pets has really helped people to keep some connection to and empathy for other living things. We hope it has, in some ways, kept alive the seed of remembering," said Stan.

"So, all this time you have been trying to communicate and not just to get treats?" laughed Jack.

"Well, I like treats too!" said Stan.

"And all other pets have been trying to communicate? Even *gerbils*?" said Jack as he rubbed the tufty hair on top of Stan's head.

"Yep, that's what I am saying," said Stan, shoving his head in Jack's face and giving him a big lick. Jack pushed him off, laughing.

"That's mad!" exclaimed Jack.

"Not when you think about it," said Stan. "I think it is why your dad wanted you to have a dog." Stan's voice was proud and gentle.

Jack's mind filled with memories of being in London, and how when his dad was in hospital, he had said he should have a puppy. It was the best thing. The city was so busy and alien to him, it had been such a comfort to take Stan to the nearby park where they would play among a group of huge plane trees. Jack felt a rush of emotion – Stan had been there through everything. He kissed his furry nose.

"I think I might need a treat," said Stan as he ran around and around in circles. Laughing, Jack rummaged in his pockets for the elusive treats.

"You're not going to get away with demanding treats, you know!"

Stan smiled his little toothy dog grin. *What would it be like if everyone could hear animals and the trees?* thought Jack; he knew it would be amazing.

A flash of movement in the trees caught Jack's eye; to one side of the glade, set back in the trees, he realised there was a group of wooden houses on stilts. A person had come out of the houses and was walking fast towards him; Jack recognised her as the same woman he had seen carry the girl away. Her dark, curly hair was streaked with grey and he could just make out that she had a tattoo or marking on her forehead. As she came closer, he gasped, as he saw she had a real snake coiled around her neck; it was beautiful, with clear, jagged, diamond-like patterns along its back. He loved snakes and had spent hours reading about them. Captivated, he stood staring as she walked towards him. The snake stared back, its red eyes piercing into him. His body tingled.

"Jack, welcome," said the woman. "The trees have talked about you and your father for many years, but they were not sure if everything would align for you to get here." Her voice was strong but kind.

He nodded slowly, lost for words.

"Please don't be afraid. I am Snakeskin. I am sorry you had to arrive to the Tree Council during a Breaking.

Things are worse than we thought – the Root Network is already growing weak. I know what you just saw with the Dark Rain was hard; it was for us all," said Snakeskin.

"Who was that girl?" asked Jack.

"Her name is Sylvie," said Snakeskin.

"What has happened to her?"

"Things are not always as we hope, Jack. She is resting; Aster and her mother are with her. We will do all we can to keep her connected. We will use herbs and ancient medicines for now to try and reduce the slow fading into forgetting," said Snakeskin.

Jack looked up into Snakeskin's eyes, relieved that she would not be cast out, knowing too well what that felt like.

"Maybe you can help her, Jack."

"What?" Jack muttered.

"Come and sit down; there is so much to tell you," she said, gesturing to a large, round, smooth rock near Taxus.

"We hope we might be able to change things for her, and all the others that have forgotten." Snakeskin's voice was thoughtful. "To introduce myself, I am the clan leader and healer. I carry ancient knowledge passed down from my mother and her mother over and over," she said.

"She is being modest," Taxus interjected. "Snakeskin is one of our greatest leaders and healers. She has been gifted with the very rare ability to travel through the Root Network to heal and to share our knowledge across the world and across the Rings of Time," she said.

"So, not just anyone can use the Root Network?" asked Jack.

"No. Tree Elders and the Earth's Protector must weave and dream the pathways across the network and through the Rings of Time," said Snakeskin. "We can access the past, or in your case, our future, but it must be prepared for, and it takes a vast concentration of energy. We can all receive the knowledge via the Root Network, but we only use it to travel in special circumstances."

"What is the Earth's Protector?" Jack asked.

"You will meet our Earth's Protector soon enough, but before that, I would like to introduce you to Lela," said Snakeskin. The snake lifted its head while keeping her gaze on Jack.

"Wow," Jack muttered under his breath. "Why do you have a snake? I love snakes – can I touch her?"

"Yes. Thank you for asking," came Lela's hiss. "Thank you for your respect." The snake's voice was soft and lyrical. Jack reached out to touch her.

"I am Lela," she said as she uncurled her body from around Snakeskin and wound herself up Jack's arm.

"*Ohhh*," he whispered, as he gently touched Lela's cool skin, captivated by her ethereal beauty.

"Lela and I share a task we must complete. We have been preparing for a long time. We support each other – she is not mine, nor I hers," said Snakeskin.

"What kind of task?" asked Jack.

"To restore the balance. It is of utmost importance that we keep Lela safe, that much I can tell you," said Snakeskin, as she reached out her arm and Lela slithered back to her.

Stan came and lay at his feet but seemed agitated; Jack noticed he kept looking up and staring towards the houses.

"Stan, are you OK?" asked Jack.

Stan didn't answer. Jack followed Stan's gaze and saw there were eyes peering out from under one of the houses, yellow piercing eyes.

"What is that under that house?" he asked.

"That's our village wolf pack – they act as our protectors and warning system," said Snakeskin.

"Are they friendly?" he whispered, his mood shifting a little.

"I hope the answer is yes," said Stan.

"It is, we support each other. They are very, very important to us," said Snakeskin.

"Like you, Stan." Jack laughed. His hand had found the wolf carving in his pocket; he held it tight.

"There is a lot to understand, Jack," hissed Lela. "In your time, people have destroyed whole forests and wiped out species, because they do not feel connected anymore, and that is now threatening us all."

"How can we stop it if it has already happened and is still happening?" asked Jack, rubbing his forehead; it felt as if his head might burst with the pressure inside.

"That is complex. The Forgetting is seeping from your time to your past, our time, increasing the destruction, ring by ring. We foresee an almighty storm, a storm that will create devastation through all the Rings of Time. But it has not happened yet, and that means there is a chance to stop it," said Lela. "We can stop it."

"How can *I* do anything?" asked Jack.

"You are special Jack, you are our hope – you did not truly forget," hissed Lela.

Jack just stared at her for a moment. "But how does that mean I can help? I don't think I can do anything," he said quietly.

"For many moons, we have been planning and weaving a web through the Root Network for a Great Fire Gathering where the most important Elders, the clan leaders, and animals from far and wide will meet. Our wisest in all forms will journey through the Root Network, through the sacred Lock, to face The Forgetting, to bring back balance, preventing the storm and the final Breaking," said Snakeskin, looking gently into Jack's eyes. "And we need you to come with us. We need you to help. We must have someone from your time who understands and cares. It is the only chance – we must make things right," said Snakeskin passionately.

"Me?"

"Yes, Jack, you, and I hope Stan too."

Above them, the rooks started cawing their night cries. Jack looked up; the light was dimming. At that moment, Aster appeared out of the trees, her eyes puffy and red from crying.

"Jack, you have met Aster, my daughter," said Snakeskin.

Jack looked at her, rather embarrassed, but Aster looked straight at him.

"Sylvie was, is, my best friend," she said with a tight voice.

"Oh," mumbled Jack. "I am sorry."

Stan went to her, wagging his tail, and fell at her feet in a big, floppy heap. Aster smiled and stroked him.

"He likes you," Jack mumbled nervously, unsure of what else to say.

"Yes, of course I like her," said Stan. "I can speak for myself, you know!"

"Oh, right, of course," he said, staring at his dog, still baffled.

Jack supressed a quiet giggle and, to his relief, Aster managed to smile as she wiped away her tears.

"How are you acting so normal?" asked Jack.

"It is normal for us," she said quietly as she sat down next to them.

A wolf howled from deep in the woods, startling Jack. Stan stood alert, looking a little nervous.

"Jack, the wolves and rooks are signalling dusk is upon us, and you must return home. There is so much more to tell you, but it's not safe for you to stay any longer. The weavings are not yet complete, and we know the Root Network is weak; anything could happen." Jack stood, shocked at the sudden mention of going home.

"There is more to explain and prepare; we need you to come back. We know it is a lot to ask, a lot to take in. The journey will be dangerous, but we need you," said Snakeskin.

"We need you," hissed Lela.

"I hope you can join us," called Taxus gently. Jack turned and looked up at the huge, dark, sentry-like tree behind them and then around to the circle of ancient trees. He breathed in slowly.

"If you cannot get up to the wood to Feya the Beech, then visit the graveyard and come to me," said Taxus. "We can both cross through deep time and the Root Network," said Taxus.

"I will always be waiting for you," said Snakeskin. "Lela's adder eyes will see you coming. She has the power of foresight, and she can hear your vibrations. She will whisper and I will be waiting."

Lela looked at Jack, and Jack felt like the look went right through him.

"But remember, sometimes what is unknown, or different, scares people, so it may be best not to share this yet," said Snakeskin.

"No chance of that," Jack mumbled. He turned to Aster, aware she was still sitting hunched over.

"Bye," he said a bit awkwardly.

Aster turned. "Bye, Jack, please come back," she said quietly, doing her best to smile.

"Feya will take you back to the wood in your time," said Taxus.

Jack had a sinking feeling. He wasn't sure he wanted to go back to his world; he felt more accepted and more welcome here than he had anywhere else before.

"Jack, hold my collar," said Stan, "and shut your eyes."

Jack obediently did as he was told, not quite believing that his dog had just given him an order. Snakeskin called, "Now!" and Jack jolted, feeling himself twisting and turning through tunnels in the dark, cool earth. He landed with a bump, back at the edge of the wood above his town. He sat for a moment, looking down the valley, his body tingling. The limbs of a dead tree were starkly silhouetted against the sky; he'd not noticed that before – how had he not seen it? There were vapour trails from planes across the sky, and cars were still whizzing along the road below. Yes, this was his world, his time, the same, but somehow now so different. The sky looked like it was late afternoon, thankfully, it was not yet dusk here, but he still knew he had been out too long. He took a deep breath and then ran off down the hill with Stan pelting ahead of him.

Chapter 3

When he and Stan tumbled through the door, Jack's mum was waiting, standing by the sink, her arms folded.

"Where have you been?" Her voice was trembling with the effort of keeping control. "I was worried. I am sure I don't need to tell you that, and that is the last thing I need right now." Her words were clipped, anger bubbling underneath.

Jack realised she looked like she might have been crying. He stared at the floor.

"Sorry, my phone has no signal in the woods," he said.

"Jack, please. I need to be able to trust you if you want to go off with Stan – you cannot go for that long."

"I'm sorry, I'm really sorry," he said.

"Do you really understand that? What were you doing for so long?" she asked.

"Um, I was just kind of wandering with Stan," he said, still avoiding eye contact.

Jack's mum cast a worried look at him. She took a breath to speak, but stopped as if she thought better of it. Stan interrupted by sitting by his dog bowl barking short, sharp *yips*. A smile flickered on Jack's face, knowing that Stan understood everything.

"Um, I think Stan's hungry," he said, turning away.

"Well, feed him then. And make sure he has water," she said.

"About time, I'm starving," muttered Stan very quietly. Jack grunted, trying to hold back his laugh.

"I'm tempted not to give you your dinner!" said his mum, smiling, attempting to lighten the mood. She held out a plate of steaming lasagne.

"Thanks, Mum," he said. "Can I eat in my room? I'm really tired."

"Are you sure you are OK?"

"I'm OK, just tired," Jack said.

Jack ate while looking out of his bedroom window. He saw the twins, Mia and Tom, playing on the trampoline in their garden by the big oak tree. *They aren't that similar for twins*, he thought. Mia was slight and slim; Tom was far bigger and taller. Jack wished things were different and that he could be playing with them, but as he watched, he noticed that Tom kept laughing and jumping so that Mia fell over, but Mia wasn't laughing, and the longer he watched, the less he was sure that she was really having fun at all.

Turning away, Jack fell into bed, exhausted and overwhelmed. Stan curled up in his usual spot right next to him and instantly started his snuffling dog snore. Jack smiled and was asleep in seconds.

The next morning, Jack was pulled from a deep dream by a lot of voices and shouting outside his window. He looked out to see people all milling around outside Mia and Tom's house. Jack ran downstairs.

"Mum, what happened?"

"There was a flood of some sort and next door's ceiling has fallen in. Luckily no one was hurt, but I think there is a lot of damage, mostly in their kitchen. I guess we should invite them over," she said.

"No!" he blurted out without thinking.

"Sorry? What?" said his mum.

"Oh, I just mean I want to take Stan for a walk. I was, er, making a, um, a den. I want to finish it…" His words trailed off.

"I know it's not the best time, but we can't be selfish. Imagine if it was you," she insisted.

"But… you can't make me," he said.

"Yes, I can," she said. With this, she turned away and carried on cooking.

"Mum, you don't understand," he said. "I can't see them!" shouted Jack.

"What do you mean you can't? Jack, this is not like you."

"Mum, they bully me!" he blurted out. He had not told his mum anything about what was going on at school with the twins. She was already so low with everything; he had just kept it in. His eyes filled with tears. Jack's mum stopped whisking the eggs.

"What do you mean?" she asked.

Jack turned away. He didn't know how to start, and the tears started rolling down his cheeks.

"Jack?" His mum looked distraught. She reached out and pulled him towards her into a hug. "You can talk to me. Why didn't you tell me?"

Jack pulled away. "I, it's OK." He tried to stuff back in the tears.

"It's not OK. Jack, what has been going on?" Her voice trembled.

Jack couldn't look her in the eye; he turned away.

Stan started walking around them in little circles and brushing up against Jack's mum's leg.

"Jack, look, Stan's filthy. Let's brush him," she said.

Jack recognised his mum's trick of finding something to do when she wanted him to talk, sideways talking as she called it, but right now he was glad of it; he couldn't hold it in anymore. They started grooming Stan's grey, messy fur, and as they did, Jack's words came tumbling out, just a few at first, then a whole torrent. Stan wagged his tail, just a little, encouraging Jack. Knowing that Stan was listening helped him tell his mum.

"They say I am weird because I like nature and know so much about plants and trees. I'm too clever, and that makes me stupid, apparently, and they call me 'Flaky' because of my eczema." He paused, biting his lip, trying to stop the tears. "I wish Dad was here."

"Jack, why haven't you told me before? I can help. We can sort it out together," she said.

Jack could see tears welling in her eyes too and started to feel bad, but that made him feel angry. Jack's mum fell silent. She reached out to hug him, but he pulled away.

"Jack," she said.

"Don't invite them over," he snapped.

They stood in silence for a moment.

"I'm not ready to see people really either," said his mum, "we won't."

Jack tried to smile.

"Please can I take Stan for a walk?" he said.

"Don't just run away to the woods with Stan. We need to talk about this."

"I'm not running away. I've told you now, haven't I? I knew you would make a fuss. You can't always fix things, Mum, please, you will just make it worse."

"Jack, that's not fair – I want to help." Her voice was wobbly, but Jack just wanted to escape.

"Please, Mum, it's a Saturday," he said.

The moment was interrupted by a bout of frantic barking from Stan. Jack shot him a swift look.

"I just want to go back to the woods; you know where I will be."

"You love those woods," she said. "Don't be so long today please."

Jack grabbed a banana and a packet of crisps from the table and shoved them in his trouser pocket. He pushed open the door, and out onto the lane. His mind was buzzing with questions, and he wanted to get back to Snakeskin and the Tree Council.

"I need a treat, for all my good work!" said Stan. "And I think your mum maybe understands more than you realise and might even be able to help if you shared more things with her."

"She won't get it," Jack snapped, still feeling angry. "Dad would have." He looked away from Stan in a grump.

The world around him was thick with new noises – could he really hear the trees murmuring as he walked by? His skin tingled, it was so amazing, but after the conversation with his mum, it also felt overwhelming. He stood still for a moment and tried to imagine that where he stood was once part of the huge forest. He wriggled his toes, picturing the root network under his feet.

Up ahead, he could see the giant yew tree silhouetted against the dark sky. A large, sleek, black crow was perched in the tree, wobbling around on the bendy branches. A distant rumble of thunder vibrated through Jack, snapping him out of his mood.

"Come on, let's see what today brings," he said, his voice more positive.

As they walked through the gate into the graveyard towards Taxus, Jack could hear a strange noise, a kind of snuffling.

"What's that?" he said.

He stopped and looked around. He couldn't see anything. Stan lifted his nose to sniff the air.

"Well, someone is nearby – I can smell them. They smell sweet, like sugar. You know, it smells like Mia from next door," said Stan, twitching his nose.

Jack's stomach tightened at the mention of her name; he looked around anxiously. Behind them, someone shouted, and Jack saw Tom running at speed, towards him and Stan.

"Mia, I'm going to find you – you best come out," came Tom's sneery voice.

He stopped suddenly and stared at Jack. "What are you doing here, Flaky?"

He started walking towards Jack and Stan, full of bravado and swagger.

"Where is she? You had better tell me if you know. She wouldn't want to be near you anyway. And get that runty mutt away from me," said Tom. His tone was one of total disdain.

Jack's mind blurred. *I will be safe with Taxus*, he thought. He grabbed Stan's collar and started to run but could hear Tom coming up behind him.

"You can't hide from me!" Tom shouted.

He ran towards the cavernous hole inside the ancient yew tree.

"Hello, Jack," called Taxus.

At that moment, Jack tripped over something, and as he fell, he landed on that something, soft but hard, and it let out a loud squeak. Simultaneously, he felt the now almost familiar jolt in his belly and was soon sliding at speed down the tree roots, deep down through the earth. This time, he kept his eyes open – it was amazing – there were so many roots and magical fungi trails, creature holes and sparkles of rocks and crystals poking through the walls of the tunnel. Just as he was getting used to the sensation, he landed with a jolt.

Chapter 4

Jack's eyes snapped open. A high-pitched shrieking was reverberating all around him. He sat up, astonished to see Mia on the ground next to him, yelling at the top of her voice. Stan was running in circles, his nose to the ground. Mia immediately started thumping Jack.

"What have you done? Where am I? What have you done, weirdo?" she shouted. Jack jumped up and Mia followed.

"I haven't done anything," he said defensively. "I don't know why *you're* here. I don't want *you* here." His voice was wobbly, but angry.

"Where am I, Jack?" Mia shouted, looking around in confusion. "What is this? What have you done?" She stood defiantly, but with her face half hidden by her long, dark fringe. Jack lent over to touch her arm reassuringly.

"Don't touch me," Mia screamed.

But something was wrong – the wood looked and felt very different. *Where are we?* thought Jack. The forest was not the same – huge swathes of trees were missing. The air was thick, and the light was odd, like dusk, but with an orange hue, not morning light. The wind was raging through the trees, the younger trees bending and swaying, but the older trees were making terrible groaning and cracking sounds. The earth felt like it was trembling too. No voices greeted him; it was eerie and strange. What had happened? Even Stan was standing right up next to Jack, looking confused, as if he didn't know where to go.

"Shhhhhh," said Jack, "listen, shhhhh, be quiet and stop yelling, you never know who you will disturb, or what!" his voice finding an unexpected force.

"What do you mean?" she whimpered, the anger turning to fear. "What's happening, Jack? What have *you* done?" she said, her voice becoming more forceful.

"I haven't done anything," said Jack.

"Where am I?" she shouted in the accusatory tone that Jack was used to.

"I don't know; maybe we've gone to a different time, OK!" he said.

"Oh, don't be stupid," she snapped. "Stop playing tricks on me. Don't you dare, you're not Tom!" She leaned forward, shouting right in Jack's face.

Stan was looking alert towards the path.

"Jack, Jack, that way," he whispered.

Jack stepped away from Mia and looked where Stan's nose pointed to. He could just make out the houses in the distance, but they looked battered. Nobody was around: no fire, no smoke and no Tree Council. Where was Snakeskin?

She had said she would always be there to meet him, but there was no sign of her. Then the earth shuddered under his feet and suddenly everything seemed to shift and tremble. The wood started appearing and disappearing before his eyes: one moment he saw shadows of buildings flickering, then the trees again, then buildings and roads, then the trees, like two worlds merging and crossing.

"Snakeskin, help!" he yelled.

Stan barked but didn't speak.

"Jack! Someone's coming, someone weird over there!" Mia shrieked.

Jack turned; Snakeskin was running towards them through the trees.

"Snakeskin!" he shouted. "What's happening? Everything keeps shifting, and I can see buildings and then the woods; it's all muddled. I'm scared."

Snakeskin's face was stern and fearful. Jack could see Lela still curled around her neck, but her red eyes were dark, carrying a deep sadness.

Mia suddenly screamed, grabbed Jack and pushed him in front of her. Her eyes fixed on Lela the Adder around Snakeskin's neck.

"Get her, and that *thing*, away from me!" Mia shrieked.

"It's OK – it's only Lela." Jack's voice held steady.

"It's a snake, Jack!" she shouted.

"Mia, shut up!" shouted Jack, pulling away from her.

Mia stood quietly, in shock.

Snakeskin nodded to Mia, but in her hurry did not speak to her.

“Jack, this is not what we planned,” said Snakeskin, breathless, focusing all her attention on Jack. “The timings have gone wrong. The network is weak, and the trees have not been able to take you to the intended time. The trees and fungi are struggling to hold the Root Network together. Jack, I told you we foresaw a terrible storm and destruction – we are at the start of that breaking time. The Forgetting is reaching out through all the Rings of Time, drawing us into her, and the rings are on the verge of collapse.”

“What do you mean? Now is a different time to yesterday?” asked Jack, still trying to keep focus.

“We were going to explain more and prepare you more, before bringing you to the time of the Great Fire Gathering, but it is all happening too fast; The Forgetting has grown too strong, so we are at that time.” Snakeskin’s voice, for the first time, was rushed and on edge. “We must hurry, come, follow me. You too,” she said, acknowledging Mia’s presence.

Jack rushed after Snakeskin, with Stan at his heels.

“Mia, come on,” he shouted.

“What’s happening? Where are we going?” spat Mia. “Get me out of here,” she shouted after him. When no one answered, she trailed after them.

“Jack, what’s gone wrong?” Stan whispered.

“I don’t know – I’m scared,” said Jack.

“Jack! We are glad to see you,” called the familiar kind, strong voice of Taxus. “You seem to have an unexpected companion, but I think she must be needed too. The network would not let just anyone come, well not normally, anyway."

Jack looked up, Taxus was standing alone, bending, and swaying in the wind, but the sleek black crow was still bobbing on one of her branches. Shadows of the Tree Council trees kept appearing then disappearing around him, and the roots below his feet were glowing slightly. Everything seemed to be in motion; Jack felt like he was on a boat, the land rocking and moving around him. His heart pounded.

"What's happening?" called Jack.

"Jack, be strong," the voice of the Tree Council echoed around him.

"But it is all muddled, everything going and coming back!" shouted Jack.

"Jack, be calm, we have to be strong," came the powerful voice of Ogham. "Keep us in your mind; hold on."

Then there was a shudder, and with relief, Jack watched as the wood and Tree Council formed around them, the rocking stopped, but the animals still seemed to be in hiding – there was none of the chatter from the birds and plants, just a low moaning and muttering and a feeling of panic in the air.

"Who is this you have with you?" asked Ogham.

"I'm sorry, I didn't mean to bring her. I tripped over her and landed on her when I fell through the Root Network, and she just seemed to come too. Her name is Mia," Jack called out, a ripple of anger evident.

"Welcome, Mia," said Ogham.

“Welcome, Mia,” said Taxus. “Mia and I have in fact met a few times – she has come to me in the graveyard, although she may not be aware of this. I do know some of your story, Mia, and maybe we can help you. Jack is not as different to you as you might think.”

Mia said nothing. She was standing like stone, her fists clenched. All the colour had drained from her skin.

“It’s OK,” said Stan, looking at Mia, “it’s the trees talking. I’m Stan,” he said, wagging his tail.

Mia stared at the dog. Jack turned to her and realised she looked like she might be sick, her expression a mixture of anger, fear and utter confusion.

“What were you doing there, inside Taxus, crying?” he asked.

Mia ignored his question and stood staring out from under her fringe. Looking at her, Jack thought how her slim body had lost its usual dominance and now looked fragile and small in this turbulent land.

“This is ridiculous; it’s a horrible trick,” she shouted, trying to sound tough. “I don’t want to be here; I want to go home. I’m nothing like Jack. You can’t hold me against my will.” She was wringing her hands as she spoke, and her voice and eyes conveyed more fear than anger.

“It is not possible for you to go home right now,” said Taxus gently. “Our energies are stretched too thin with trying to hold the Root Network together; I am afraid we don’t have the power to get you back just now. Instead, we must move forward, and get you prepared for the journey ahead,” her voice firm, but kind and parental in tone.

"What journey? You can't make me do anything. I'm not going anywhere other than home." Mia's voice was becoming quieter, less forceful.

"Jack is going to have to explain to you what he can; we are short of time. I am sorry – it will be a lot to take in. The fact that you can hear us now means you too have not fully forgotten. We need you, Mia, we need you to help us," said Taxus.

Mia made a strange noise: half grunt, half huff.

"But what is going on?" asked Jack. "Everything keeps going all strange, like I am seeing another world. Why do the Tree Council keep appearing and disappearing?"

"You are seeing the Rings becoming weak, Jack," called Taxus across the wind. "Everything is crossing over and becoming jumbled; our strength is waning. It is what we feared, the collapse of the Rings of Time and the Root Network, systems faltering. Too much destruction means that The Forgetting has grown too strong. We have so little time left," Taxus said solemnly.

Around them, the wind was getting stronger; leaves and branches were spinning through the air. Stan started barking frantically.

"I don't like it, Jack!" Stan called.

"Me neither," said Jack quietly.

"Jack, touch my bark," called Feya, "and, Mia, you too, it will help you to understand."

Jack walked over and put his hand on Feya's bark and felt his mind calm. Mia stood defiantly, not moving.

"Quick, come inside," called Snakeskin, heading up

the steps to one of the houses. She held out her hand to Mia, who refused it and turned away. Jack grabbed Mia's arm and started pulling her along. She stumbled after him.

"You have to come," he said urgently.

Stan ran in front as Jack and Mia staggered up the creaky steps to the house. Inside, the house was dilapidated and bare, just some old wooden beds covered with dried bracken. The light was dim, but at least it was warmer out of the wind. Jack sat down on one of the beds. Mia sat next to him, with an icy distance between them.

"Snakeskin, what's happening? Where is everyone? Why is everything broken?" asked Jack.

"Things are starting to decay as the Rings falter. Many of the clan have gone ahead to prepare for a Great Fire Gathering, where we must go too. Aster and I have stayed behind to travel with you; we have been gathering some tools for you and some gifts from the trees. We will have to explain everything on the journey now; we are running out of time," said Snakeskin.

Mia sat silent, scuffing her trainers on the floor. From deep in the wood, there was the haunting screech from a fox. Mia flinched; her knuckles gripped the bed. Jack was aware that Stan was not speaking. He looked at him.

"What is it?" he whispered.

"Well, I'm not sure she's ready! It might all be a bit much," said Stan.

"We don't have time for her not to be ready," said Jack. He felt a strange confidence surging through him.

Then Mia suddenly spoke. "What is this place? It seems like you know everyone here," her voice sullen and sharp.

"It's a long story; I don't know really. I came here yesterday, somehow, with Stan. It's new to me too, you know. I met these trees known as the Tree Elders, called Ogham, Feya and, of course, Taxus, but yesterday I was in a different place or time, and it looked different somehow. I also started hearing trees and animals talk – the trees have told me that the world is collapsing because people have forgotten how to talk to trees and animals, and so we need to help change the future, kind of. If we don't, The Forgetting will destroy everything," said Jack, looking at Stan. "Just a normal day." He tried a weak smile, knowing that it all sounded crazy.

"Yep, that's right," said Stan. "You don't know how long I have been trying to get him to hear me! My tail hurts from wagging so much!" said Stan, gently laughing. "And Conker, your cat, she's so frustrated that you just won't listen. It's been tough for us pets. Sometimes we think humans are a bit stupid, but now we know it's not your fault."

Mia looked at Stan and managed a small smile, her bewilderment dropping for a moment. It was quite cool hearing Stan speak.

"Conker? Really?" she asked, her voice a little softer.

"Yes, Conker, she's OK for a cat," said Stan.

While the wind raged outside and Snakeskin and Aster were busy packing, Jack and Stan did their best to try and explain, at speed, what they knew.

Chapter 5

There was a loud crash. Jack ran outside, Stan close behind. In front of him was a fallen beech tree, its roots now poking up like an upturned beetle. He took a breath, relieved it wasn't Feya. The trees around were emitting a low, moaning noise, like an ancient weeping. Jack stood staring. Then, Taxus let out a huge roar, like a war cry.

"Trees!" she called. "Hold firm. We *must* use our force. Use all your energy to keep together, and do not let fear take your strength. This time it will be different. Tree Council, we have prepared long and hard for this; it is our only chance. It is time to face the storm."

Jack looked in awe at Taxus, so ancient, tall and defiant, her dark branches blowing in the wind.

"Quickly!" called Aster. "Come back inside – we must get our things."

"Now!" shouted Snakeskin.

Jack and Stan headed back inside. Mia was standing

waiting by the door, biting her nails. The sleek, black crow, who had been sitting on a branch of Taxus, flew down through the open door, carrying something in its beak. He flew past them and landed on one of the wooden beds.

"I am Mede," he said. "I have brought you some medicines gathered from the trees and plants. We do not know what will be left where you are going, so you will need to carry this on your journey." He dropped a small pouch on the bed and perched with his head on one side. Aster walked over and opened it. Jack looked from Mia to Snakeskin to Aster.

"Hello," said Jack.

Mede held his eyes on Jack. Jack was taken aback by the deep gaze of the crow. Mede started listing everything from the pouch.

"Willow bark, for pain relief, willow holds the lunar knowledge. Oak bark to make an astringent to help a fever or if there is any infection. Cleavers as a tonic if you are ill. Lime blossom makes a good reviving tea. Snakeskin has made a tonic from hornbeam bark, which will help relieve tiredness and exhaustion. And here are some hornbeam leaves – they are good for a bad cut – they help to stop the bleeding."

At this statement, Jack caught Mia's eye. His hands felt sweaty and cold. He started scratching at his eczema again.

"My mum always told me to be careful of wild plants," snapped Mia.

"Yes," said Mede, calmly staring at Mia with his bright

eyes. "You must always know exactly what it is you are picking, and learn from those who know," said Mede. "You see for us, we ask the plants, and they tell us if they are safe to eat or good medicine; they never lie. Your time is different, and it is part of The Forgetting that people don't trust the plants. You will soon learn again what healing is possible. What I am giving you is safe," said Mede. His intelligent eyes looked from Jack to Mia.

"Thank you," said Jack. He felt his tummy fluttering with nerves, the reality of the journey sinking in.

"I will be glad to come with you as your teacher and guide," said Mede, tilting his head again.

"Oh, yes," said Jack quietly. "Thank you, that would be amazing." He had an instant liking for the crow.

Mia sat staring. Stan walked to Mede and put his nose close to the bird's beak. They both nodded to each other. Mede then bowed his head and perched quietly as Aster helped to put the herbs in Mia's rucksack, saying the names of each one again. Mia still just watched, refusing to take part. Aster caught Mia's eye, then silently left, saying nothing.

"Do you have anything with you?" asked Snakeskin, interrupting.

Jack turned and started rummaging in his pockets, pulling things out one by one.

"A penknife, a torch, dog treats."

Stan's ears pricked up. "Dog treats, did you say?"

"And my phone, but don't think the battery is going to last long."

At the mention of a phone, Mia suddenly started fumbling in her coat pocket for her own and looked at it hopefully, as if it could somehow connect her to a world she knew, but there was of course no signal, and in fact, the phone didn't function at all. She stared at it for a moment. Then she delved in her small backpack, and pulled out a pen, a diary and a lighter.

"Why have you got that?" asked Jack, pointing at the lighter.

Mia looked down and bit her lip. "We were going to have a bonfire and a barbeque, but we didn't." Her voice was quiet, and she stuttered a bit. "It was all my fault. I left the taps running."

Of course. Her house had been flooded that morning, he had almost forgotten, it seemed so long ago.

"Oh, not good," said Stan.

Mia jumped when he spoke, but he walked over and laid his head on her lap. She softened and sat stroking his head.

"That is why I went to the churchyard," said Mia. "Everyone was furious. The ceiling partly fell in; the kitchen was flooded; and Tom's phone and computer got wet and were ruined. He was so angry and started screaming at me and hitting me. My dad started shouting at me too; it always seems to be my fault, so I ran out."

"Oh god," said Jack, wincing.

For the first time, Mia looked him in the eye. He did actually feel sorry for her. He tried to smile.

"You know, Tom was trying to find you when I tripped over you. I was running away from him too."

Mia flinched. "Even so, I still want to go home," she said.

"Me too, right now, but we don't seem to have that option," said Jack.

An awkward silence followed. Stan broke the silence. "And he called me runty," said Stan. "So rude."

Jack sniggered and Mia managed a half smile.

Aster reappeared with a bag full of all kinds of objects.

"The trees have gifted you these items to help you on the journey," said Aster. "Here are some roasted beech nuts. They will be good food if in need, but don't eat too many at once; just use them for emergency energy. I keep them in my pocket." Jack held them in his hand, and nibbled at one – they were bitter. He winced as his mouth went dry.

"Wow, I think I might have to be very hungry," he muttered.

Out of the corner of his eye, Jack saw Snakeskin watching them for a moment before she left the hut.

"Lime has gifted you rope made from her bark," Aster continued, handing some thick fibrous green rope to Jack. He ran his fingers down the rope – it felt strong and pliable. He put it in his pocket.

Aster then passed him a knife.

"Taxus gifted the wood for this knife. I made it; yew wood is strong but not brittle."

Jack took the knife carefully, studying the carvings along the handle; symbols of some kind. It was exquisite. He held it rather uncertainly; would he really need it?

"Here is a mallet made from ash. Ash is hard but absorbs blows without shattering. I've added some rope to it, so you can carry it on your belt. Dancer the Ash has also gifted you this small piece of ash wood to carry, to ward off the bad energy."

Jack and Mia put the thin, knobbly ash wood in their pockets.

"And Mia, Ogham wants you to have this knife – it is made from oak and flint – my brother made it," said Aster as she handed it to Mia.

Mia took it and sat, silently tracing the delicate spiral carving on the handle.

"But I don't want to be here," said Mia, her voice quiet. "Why don't you get it? I don't want to go wherever it is we are going," she said, her anger rising. "I want to go home. Don't you get it? Why won't you listen?" she shouted.

"I know, but we can't," said Jack. "It's not that simple, and maybe this is our chance to help stop all the destruction, pollution and storms in our world. We *have* to do this," he said.

"Oh, saving the world. We are not in a film, Jack. What can *we* do?" she snapped.

"Maybe we can do something." Jack's voice had a new-found confidence. "Mia, you have started to hear the trees and animals, like I can, so maybe that means we can do something. You wouldn't cut down a tree if you could hear it talk, would you? It would change everything! Think of all the habitats being destroyed, think of all the stuff about the burning forests, what if people could hear orangutans and other animals speak or hear the trees speak, they wouldn't do it, would they? It would be like killing a person. We have to help the soul of the earth and stop The Forgetting."

The door banged open as Snakeskin came rushing in, interrupting Jack's passionate speech. She was carrying something.

"Aster, quickly. It's hurt!"

Mia's curiosity got the better of her, and she peered over at the chestnut-flecked bird in Snakeskin's hands. The bird's beady eyes locked onto her own frightened ones; she gasped at the intensity of its stare.

"What is it?" she asked, a note of awe in her voice.

"It's a young hawk," said Aster. "We don't often find them on the ground or injured; they are way too brilliant at flying for that."

The bird's eyes were still piercing and alert.

"Are you badly hurt?" asked Snakeskin.

"I am OK," the hawk responded. "Just weak. I was picked up by a strong gust and swirled into a branch, and then I fell. This wind is not normal. My wing is bruised; I can feel it. My name is Ayah."

Snakeskin quickly felt the wing and took some powdered herbs from the decorated pouch around her neck. She rubbed them into the bird's wing, then turned to Mia.

"Mia, Ayah won't be able to fly for a while. Could I ask you to look after her? She will be safe in your big coat pocket, and you will make good companions I feel." Without waiting for an answer, Snakeskin gently placed the bird in Mia's hands. Mia looked down at it cautiously, but as she peered into the bird's eyes, her stance softened. Snakeskin's own eyes flickered with a quiet knowing.

"Yes," said Mia softly, her stance changing almost instantly, "I would like that."

Aster made a nest from some cloth and then carefully placed Ayah into Mia's deep pocket so that just her head poked out. Aster reached down and stroked the bird's head.

Chapter 6

Snakeskin hoisted onto her back what looked like a bundle of branches, and Aster pulled on her bag of supplies. They stepped out of the house, back into the strange, vibrating, fluctuating world, that was veering between the dark-green forest and swirling, dusty desolation.

"Jack!" called Taxus, her voice echoing as if it was far away.

Jack looked around in fear, then the trees started to shake into view again.

"Jack," called Ogham. "Be strong; remember us; we are here."

Jack blinked, took a deep breath and the trees started to form as solid shapes again. The world fixed around him with all the Tree Council standing in their ancient circle.

"I don't like this," said Jack.

"Nor do any of us," said Stan.

"Jack," came the strong voice of Ogham. "This may just

be the most important journey of your life. Your father's teachings have prepared you well. Mia and Aster will be your companions and of course Snakeskin, Stan, Lela, and now Mede the Crow and Ayah the Hawk. They will guide you to the Lock. It is dangerous, but Lela and Snakeskin are the best guides you could have. Jack, remember you give us hope, and you, Mia," said Ogham passionately.

"What's the Lock?" asked Jack.

"It is an ancient pathway. Snakeskin and Lela will have to explain on the journey, we do not have time now, you must leave. It's important you get to the Lock before The Forgetting starts oozing through the cracks," said Ogham.

"We cannot miss our chance," called Taxus. "If we fail, the Root Network will not be strong enough. The imbalance will destroy us all," she said.

Jack looked around him, feeling a heavy responsibility; he felt small and insignificant. He touched the knife and mallet tied to his belt for some kind of strength. Mia stood silent and sullen, and she no longer looked like the bully Jack knew.

"We must go now!" said Snakeskin "What we do not have, we cannot take," she said. There was a hint of fear crackling through her normally steady voice.

Lela held her head up and looked ahead.

"We are with you," called the Tree Council in unison.

A large she-wolf appeared from under Snakeskin's house. The other wolves looked on from under the house, their eyes glinting. Mia flinched and stopped. Wolf paused and nodded a greeting at them. Mia looked down and shrank away. Stan stood behind her leg, and Jack turned and mouthed, "She's friendly. Stan, it's OK." Wolf calmly walked over, bent her head and touched Stan's nose. Stan lowered his head. Wolf then raised her eyes and looked gently into Mia's eyes.

"Wolf will lead," said Snakeskin calmly.

They set off into the stormy forest, a strange party: Wolf, Snakeskin, Lela the Adder, Aster, Jack, Mia, Ayah the Hawk – still safe in Mia's pocket – Mede the Crow – flying above – and Stan, as always at Jack's heels. The light was dim with a strange orange hue. They followed Wolf, twisting and turning along ancient paths. As they walked, Snakeskin stooped to pick plants, pushing them into her bag. Wolf stopped every so often to leave a scent mark, and Stan started doing the same, cocking his leg at every opportunity. Jack laughed at first at Stan's seriousness, but then his mind drifted back to old fairy tales, and he too started picking up stones and distinctive sticks and leaving them in strategic places. Inside, he doubted the markers would stay put in the stormy conditions, but maybe the scent might last.

The further they walked, the more tangled and overgrown the path became: creepers, old thick vines and brambles making it hard going and almost impenetrable. They scrambled and crawled along low animal paths, branches whacking them and scratching their faces. Jack grimaced; he could feel his and Mia's irritation growing. They scrambled on in silence; even Stan had stopped his usual antics. They came to a small clearing and paused for a moment. Jack saw Mia put her hand into her pocket and gently stroke Ayah's small head, and as she did, he thought he saw her relax a bit. He was glad she had the bird as a companion.

They walked on, finding themselves in amongst huge trees; the forest felt very ancient and untouched. Jack took a big breath, feeling less entangled and more comfortable with these great old trees. Snakeskin stopped and put her hand on the trunk of a large ash tree; it looked to Jack like it swayed in response. But Snakeskin dropped her head as if in sorrow, and then she walked on in total silence. They all followed. Jack suddenly saw the reason for Snakeskin's sadness: the forest came to an abrupt stop. In front of them was a vast landscape of tree stumps, as far as they could see. It was bleak and grey. There were no birds, very few plants and it was eerily silent, nothing spoke, there was just the sound of the wind droning through the stumps; it was creepy and cold. Snakeskin looked around in confusion; it was as if she had lost her compass. She looked at Wolf, who returned a quiet stare, then nodded and set off, leading the way, weaving through the bleak landscape. Snakeskin laid her hand on the stumps she passed; Jack could see her whispering something to them; he couldn't hear what was said, but her eyes were full of tears.

Lela broke the silence. "It is already happening, desolation beyond imagining. The Forgetting cannot stop; the balance has gone," hissed Lela. "We must hurry. We must get to the Lock, and for that we need to be prepared.

You must know, it is called the Gebo Lock; it is not so far – it is in the forest ahead."

"But what exactly is a Lock?" asked Jack.

"Locks are a kind of doorway in the Root Network," hissed Lela gently. "They lead to paths that will take us through the Rings of Time. They have been created by the Elders, the earth and the rocks. They have been kept secret and are only to be used for gatherings in time of great emergency; the entrances are hidden and only revealed when the need is great. My eyes can see the Locks across the earth, so I know where they stand."

"That is a gift indeed," said Snakeskin. "Not many can."

"I will guide you." Lela's gentle voice was calm and graceful. "Passing through a Lock is not easy though; you must be ready and stay focused. Once through the Lock, we will cross to the land of Eye."

"Mede," called Snakeskin. Mede swooped down to fly lower. "Please fly ahead, check our path and see what lies before us; this barren world is not one I know."

"Of course," said Mede, and he flew up and out across the stumps.

They walked on, Wolf still leading, following in the direction Mede had flown. Finally, they made it through the old stumps and back into the forest. Jack felt himself relax a little, being amongst familiar trees again; he had hated the barren land of stumps. Then, they heard it before they saw it, the beautiful sound of a running stream – it was tumbling down the hill in front of them, flowing through and over large, green, mossy boulders; it felt magical. They ran and plunged their hands into the cool, clear water, gulping large handfuls. A family of red squirrels watched from a nearby tree.

"Where is Mede?" asked Jack.

"He will be back soon," said Snakeskin. "Maybe it is further than I thought."

Lela slithered quietly from around Snakeskin's neck, along the earth to Jack and up his arm. He watched, transfixed. Mia recoiled, not quite as violently as she had when she had first seen the snake, but she still shuffled further down the log.

"She really is OK. There's nothing to be afraid of," said Aster, touching Mia's arm.

Mia jumped. "OK, OK! I'm just not used to talking snakes," said Mia and laughed awkwardly.

"But a talking dog is OK?" said Stan, wagging his tail.

Aster laughed too.

Ayah poked her head out of Mia's pocket. "And a talking bird!"

"Oh OK!" She laughed, and they all laughed.

"I am getting better, I think," said Ayah, who was studying Mia with her bright eyes.

"We cannot linger; we must move on," said Snakeskin. "We have to get to the Lock before nightfall." She held out her arm, and Lela slithered up it and curled back around her neck. Jack looked at Mia with his best 'positive' face.

"Well, at least it's more fun than kicking about bored at home." He tried a smile. Mia turned away, ignoring him.

Suddenly, Lela lifted her head from Snakeskin's

shoulder and hissed a loud warning, seeing something the others could not. The squirrels instantly scattered, and there was a thunderous rumbling and cracking sound. The earth seemed to emit a loud shriek and, in front of them, a tree came crashing down. Small splits started appearing in the ground, and the stream started gushing and frothing out of the rocks, as if the water was boiling. A strange, grey substance started to ooze slowly from the holes in the earth, its tendrils curling into the air. "Run," called the trees around them, in pained tones. Mede swooped down from high above.

"You must go down the hill to get to the Lock."

"Quick!" shouted Snakeskin. "We need to get through before The Forgetting splits out. We cannot get caught up in the Breaking. Run!" Her voice was shrill and urgent.

Snakeskin, Wolf, and Mede lead the way down the hill, with Aster behind. Jack, Stan and Mia followed them. Cracks were appearing all around them and suddenly, with a loud ripping sound, a huge cavity opened in the ground, separating Jack and Mia from the others. And it kept growing. Jack started to run along the edge, but Stan let out a loud cry. Jack looked back – Stan was yelping and tugging his leg, which was caught in one of the holes.

"Jack!" came the shriek-like bark from Stan.

Jack could see what looked like a vine or a root twisting around Stan's back leg; he saw a shimmer of silver, as if the vine had silver sap. He ran over and grabbed Stan's forelegs, trying to pull him away from the root.

"It won't break!" Jack shouted over the rumbling and cracking sounds. "Mia, help!"

Mia pulled at the knife in her pocket. Snakeskin looked on in horror. The distance between her, Jack and the dog was now too great to cross.

"Mia, Jack, you must cut it! Cut the vine, or it will pull him down. It carries a poison from The Forgetting. Mia, quickly!" Snakeskin yelled, her voice now urgent and penetrating. Jack scrabbled for the rope in his pocket and tied it around Stan's body so that he had both the collar and the rope to hold onto Stan with.

Stan's eyes were bulging with fear. "Help me – I'm slipping in, help," he cried.

Mia fumbled with the knife, her hands shaking, and she started frantically cutting at the root. Jack hung on with all his might to Stan.

"It's not cutting!" shouted Mia.

"Oh, Stan! Snakeskin, what do we do?" Jack shrieked.

"Keep cutting. Don't give up!" Snakeskin yelled over the sounds of the splitting and crashing trees.

Mia carried on sawing at the vine. Lela let out a loud hiss, and the grey tendrils recoiled but didn't let go. Ayah wriggled free from Mia's pocket and hopped down onto the vine, sinking her talons deep into its fibres. There was an unexpected loud, chilling, fox-like scream from the vine. It twisted, then recoiled back into the hole. As it let go, Stan and Jack flew backwards, landing in a heap on the ground. Jack held Stan tight to his body, his breathing coming in hard, short gasps. Mia ran to them, placing one hand on Stan, stroking him gently. Ayah flew and landed on Mia's shoulder. She wobbled a little, tentatively stretching out her wing.

"Jack, Mia, don't stop! You must try and get through," yelled Snakeskin from the other side of the massive crater. "We must get away quickly. Mia, Ayah will have to help show you the path to the Lock; I cannot get back to you!"

"Yes, I can fly better now," came Ayah's determined reply.

"We will meet you at the Lock, but you need to keep connected to us," Snakeskin shouted across the gaping chasm. "Wolf will howl, and it is important that you keep thinking about us; keep us in your mind as that will help us stay connected."

Jack picked up Stan, stumbling under the weight of him. He held Stan tight to his chest as he and Mia zigzagged through the crevices away from the grey, gooey mist, but the only route out lead them further and further from Snakeskin and the others.

"Thank you," whispered Stan with the last of his energy. He then flopped in Jack's arms, his head lolling. As Jack ran, he kept looking down at his dog, tears welling in his eyes. There was no clear path; they had to scramble through the broken and chaotic woodland. The further they went, the fainter and fainter the howls from Wolf became. Stan was heavy; Jack kept tripping and stumbling, his legs weak and wobbly. Sweat was pouring down his forehead, but he knew he couldn't stop. Ayah flew ahead, trying to keep a sense of the path.

"I'm not sure I can keep going at this pace," mumbled Jack.

Mia nodded in agreement, too out of breath to speak.

"I can't hear Wolf anymore," he shouted, "and I am not sure I can see them in my head!"

They stopped near to a large hawthorn tree. Mia was bent over, trying to catch her breath. Jack stood panting, staring at his limp dog. For a moment, they stood and listened. Nothing. Jack looked around; at least they were away from the grey mists, the terrible rupturing ground and falling trees. But before they had caught their breath, there was an immense cracking noise, and Jack felt himself falling. He tumbled and twisted and, from somewhere far away, he heard Mia scream. Then he hit the hard earth, and Stan landed awkwardly on his lap. The jolt took his breath away, and a pain seared through his chest. Winded, Jack gasped and gasped for breath, panic rising within him. From somewhere above, Mia shrieked, "Jack, Jack!"

He struggled to take a breath; he couldn't reply. He felt dizzy and muddled. His eyes went hazy; his mind turned black; he fainted.

Chapter 7

Stan wriggled on Jack's lap, jolting him 'awake'. He felt cold, the damp earth pressing into his back. For a moment, he didn't know where he was. He tried to move, but Stan was lying on him, heavy, floppy and quiet. Jack looked up and saw the steep sides of the hole rising up around him, like the sides of a well, and way above him, through the opening, he could just see the sky.

"Stan, Stan!" he shrieked.

Stan's eyes flickered and half opened.

"Jack," he whispered.

"Stan, I thought you were dead. Are you OK?" Jack asked.

"Jack, where are we?" said Stan.

"I don't know," he said, and promptly yelled, "Help!" up to the sky.

Stan suddenly dropped back down again on Jack's lap.

"Stan, what's wrong? Stan, wake up!"

"I'm ill, Jack, something's burning inside of me," said

Stan, whispering. "I can feel it in my blood." Then he went quiet.

"Stan!" Jack cried out and gently shook his dog. Stan's eyes stayed closed.

"Help! Mia! Help!" he screamed.

No one responded. He lay Stan down and quickly looked around him. The light was very dim. He touched the walls – they were cold and rough with sharp stones and twisted roots poking through. He reached up and grabbed at the sides, trying to climb up, but slithered straight back down; there was just nothing to hold onto. He took out his knife from his pocket; the carvings on the handle glinted, catching his eye for a moment. "Please help me," he whispered to the knife as he tried cutting a foothold in the wall, but the wall crumbled when he tried to hold on, and he slipped back down.

"Help! Mia, I can't get out," he yelled once more. Again, there was no answer.

Jack crawled around, prodding and poking the earth. He saw a little hole and pushed at it. The earth fell away, revealing a small tunnel.

"Stan!" he kept shouting. "Help! Snakeskin, Lela, Mia, help!" he called, but no one responded. He turned to Stan.

"Stan, I can't climb out," he whispered into his dog's ear. "I can't climb out; I have to see what's through the burrow."

Stan's ear twitched as if in recognition. Suddenly, his little mouth opened. "Jack, I am thirsty – I must drink," his voice so quiet it was almost inaudible.

Jack looked around – he had no water, nothing. He looked at the roots and wondered. He pulled out his knife again and touched a small, long, bendy root. As he did, the spiral and triangular symbols on the knife's handle started to glow. It reminded Jack of how the roots of the Tree Council had glowed under the ground.

"May I have some sap," he asked the root quietly. "Stan needs water."

The root twitched, and the symbols on his knife grew stronger. Jack carefully made a small slice in the root and lifted up Stan, so his mouth was under the slice, and the liquid dropped out onto his tongue. Stan drank the sweet sap, and his eyes opened a little.

"Clever," Stan said quietly.

Jack sat holding his dog for a moment. "Stan, no one is coming to save us; I have to go and find a way out," said Jack, lying Stan down again. "I'll be back really soon."

Lying Stan gently onto the earth, Jack started to dig frantically at the small hole in the wall. He took the mallet he'd been gifted by the trees and scrabbled and bashed at the cold soil until he made a hole that was just big enough to wriggle through on his belly. He twisted to fit his shoulders through the gap and squirmed out into a small, underground cavern. With his shoulders hunched over, he could just stand up. Above him was a maze of roots, which made a canopy, and there was some light coming from a tiny hole. He reached out with his fingertips to touch the roots, but a jolt went through his arm, like a static electric shock. He flinched and withdrew his hand. He peered at the roots, then tentatively reached up again. This time, as he touched a root, it curled, like it was responding to his touch. He gently felt along the root; Ogham had said the Root Network was all around him, so, while touching the root, he called out, "Help, help me. Ogham, Feya, Taxus, trees, help me."

Would the Root Network carry his voice to them? He called back through the hole, "Stan, I'll get us out. Hang on! Please, don't die." His voice trailed off.

Jack waited a moment, then he started feeling his way around the cavern. He traced his fingers along deep groves in the walls; they felt like scratches. His mind spun – what had made them? A strong, sour odour filled his nostrils; a shiver rippled down his spine. He reached up again and touched the tree root, hoping something would change. A tinkling noise rang out. He shook his head – was it in his head or in the chamber? He couldn't be sure; then a voice echoed around him: "Jack, follow the footprints; be strong; we are with you."

He looked around the gloom; the voice sounded familiar. He had to do something. He got down on his hands and knees and started crawling along the floor, feeling his way with his outstretched hand. There seemed to be two tunnel pathways: one felt more worn, and definitely smelled stronger, but he didn't know which was the right way to go? He peered up both tunnels and could just see a large, black beetle scuttling ahead of him. It stopped and seemed to look at him – was it trying to help? He had no other clues, so started crawling along the tunnel behind it. He turned and yelled over his shoulder: "Stan, we are going to get out – don't give up."

The words 'we are with you, Jack' seemed to be reverberating down the tunnel. Was his mind playing tricks? He crawled on, determined, but fear was pounding in his chest; he was getting further and further from Stan. The black beetle stopped and seemed to wait for him for a moment, as if it wanted to be sure he was following, then it scuttled on. It was getting harder to see; his confidence was wavering; he felt so alone. He was so conflicted, he looked over his shoulder – should he leave Stan? As he turned to look ahead, he came nose to nose with a large, black-and-white face. He jumped and bumped his head on the ceiling of the tunnel.

"We came as quick as we could," came the deep, gravelly voice of a large badger, "as soon as the trees started whispering about you being trapped. We had left this den when the fractures started."

"Oh, hello, you're friendly, phew," said Jack.

"I most definitely am friendly to any friend of Snakeskin and the Tree Council," said the badger. "We heard you need help. Are you OK?"

"I'm OK, but Stan is very ill, and he is back in the den. How do I get him out?" asked Jack.

"We will have to dig," said the badger. "We must hurry."

It was then he saw that just behind, there was a second badger.

"I am Steel, and this is Grey," said the first badger.

"We must get back to Stan," said Jack. The knot of tight

fear in his belly hurt. He couldn't turn around, so started wriggling awkwardly backwards down the tunnel. The two great beasts followed.

*

Mia was lying in the silence, her head dropping down the edge of the hole, staring in shock into the darkness. All she could see were steep sides disappearing into the gloom. There was no way down and no way out.

"Jack," she yelled again and again.

Standing up, she stared into the woods around her. The dark shapes and shadows of the trees loomed over her, creeping towards her. Creaks and rustles came from every direction. She couldn't hear Wolf or any voices from afar. Her mouth went dry. She looked up, hoping to see Ayah way up in the sky, but even the sky was empty. Had Ayah seen what had happened or was she too far ahead trying to find the path? Mia knew she was alone. She crumpled down with her back against the hawthorn tree, fighting back tears.

"I want to go home," she said out loud.

The leaves above her rustled. "Are you sure?" came a low voice. Mia jumped up and looked around. "Mia, do you really want to go home?"

"Who are you?" she said quietly.

"We are The Fungi; we connect to the Root Network."

"Right," she said grumpily. "I can't do this; I want to go home. What can I do now? They've gone, all of them. I never asked to be here."

"If you are sure. Our energy is stretched, but here we can try – it is one of the last places where we can maybe still make the connection to the Root Network in your time. If you are sure, we can take you home, if that's what you really want."

"Of course it is what I want," she said firmly.

"Just push your toes into the soil by the tree roots, and we will use the last of our strength to get you home," said Fungi.

Mia took off her shoes and placed her feet on the cool earth, but she did not dig her toes in. She sat for a moment, staring at her feet, her hands pressed hard into the soil.

"Home, yes," she said quietly, as if to herself.

She felt for her knife and held it in her hands. The handle started to glow. She stared at it and, as she did, her head filled with images of Jack somewhere in the dark earth. It was like her mind could see them somewhere underground. She shook her head, trying to rid herself of the thought. Was he alive? Was Stan alive?

"Jack, Stan, where are you?" she shouted into the darkness.

But there was no reply.

"We must go if you are ready; we do not have much time – there may be another Breaking," came the firm voice of Fungi.

She looked around her, looked at the trees, who no longer loomed at her like shadow fiends. She stared into the darkness and turned the knife in her hands.

"No!" she suddenly shouted. "I can't leave; I can't leave Jack and Stan here."

She jumped up and shouted, "Jack," repeatedly into the darkness. All around, the trees rustled, and she was sure she heard a tinkling sound coming from near the hawthorn tree. Then, from high above her, she heard a high-pitched *puewwwee* sound. Looking up, she saw Ayah hurtling towards her from the sky.

*

Deep in the earth, the badgers were digging and digging with their huge, powerful paws and claws. Alongside, Jack was scrabbling at the earth with his bare hands.

"Be careful," said Steel the Badger. "We do not want to make the hole too big, or it will collapse. Hawthorn, we need you to help us," he called, turning his voice to the ancient hawthorn tree above them.

"Of course," came the soft tones of the hawthorn's overhead voice. "I am so sorry I couldn't speak to you before, Jack, there are now dark patches that appear in the Root Network, which stop us communicating. The best I could do was tingle my roots and say a few words to try and help you know you were not alone. I asked Beetle to help."

"Thank you for the sap," said Jack.

"You are most welcome, Jack, it was something I could do."

"Stan, we are coming. I have help. We will be safe," Jack shouted, willing his dog, his best friend, to be OK.

He heard a strange gurgling sound, and he crawled ahead to Stan, while the badgers dug and dug behind him, their huge claws making it look easy.

"Stan, I have met some badgers, and the hawthorn tree is here." Stan was lying on his side, his eyes flickering, a little froth at the edge of his mouth. "Stan, don't die on me!" commanded Jack, biting his cheeks to hold his tears back. He reached for the root and dropped some more of the liquid into Stan's mouth. Stan stirred.

"Quickly," called Steel, "we must pull him out gently."

"Here, put him on my shirt," said Jack, awkwardly squirming around to get his T-shirt off over his head. He gently picked up Stan and laid him onto it. Steel held onto the front with his teeth, while Grey held on to the back with hers, and Jack wriggled alongside, helping to lift Stan. Slowly, they manoeuvred Stan through the hole into the cavern.

A sudden shrill shouting echoed from above them. "Jack, Jack, Jack! Where are you?" It was Mia's voice.

"I'm here," yelled Jack. "I'm underground, in a badger's den, we're coming. Mia, wait there!"

All was quiet again. Jack wasn't sure she'd heard. They carried on, pushing, pulling and wiggling Stan along the tunnel. The light grew stronger; the air changed; the pungent smell became weaker.

"Mia, Mia! Snakeskin!" Jack yelled again.

Suddenly, Jack saw hands reaching in, scrabbling at the earth above him.

"Jack, is that you? Oh Jack!" Mia yelled, her hands feeling for him.

"Mia, Stan is very ill – I need Snakeskin!" he yelled, his voice hoarse and shrill.

"Jack, it is Mede, I am here too," came the cawing voice. "I came as soon as I heard what had happened; we have been trying to reach you. Snakeskin and the others are trying to find a way to get here, but it is a long way around," said the crow.

The two badgers and a very muddy Jack finally emerged out of a tunnel into the light, next to the thin and twisted trunk of the old hawthorn tree.

"Oh, Jack, Stan!" Mia fell onto her knees next to them and started stroking the limp body of the dog. Ayah hopped around on the earth next to them, watching.

"We must get help, Mede, now! Stan said something about his blood burning. Where is Snakeskin?" Jack's voice was frantic.

"She is stuck on the other side of the huge ravine. Jack, let me see – show me the wound," said Mede.

The badgers stood to one side, as Jack lifted Stan onto his lap and held his head, stroking his muddy fur. Mede, the sleek, black crow, perched next to Stan and surveyed the now red and swollen lump on his leg.

"That is ancient poison – it carries The Forgetting's festering energy. We must remove it; I fear for him. Jack, Mia you must make a fire now, immediately," said Mede firmly.

Jack lay Stan down gently on some soft grass at the base of the hawthorn tree. His hands were shaking as he rummaged in his pack for the birch bark Mede had given them at the start of the journey.

"Mia, I need your lighter and some twigs," said Jack, thankful for all the fires he'd made with his dad. Ayah immediately flew off and came back with some small twigs in her beak. Jack and Mia hastily cleared a little patch of earth away from the tree and made a small fire. They blew and blew on the tiny flame until it caught, and the twigs started to burn.

"Keep putting small amounts of wood on it, Mia," instructed Jack with more confidence in his voice than he felt inside.

Mede then perched gently on Stan's leg.

"Stan, this may hurt, and for that I am sorry, but I must get the poison out," said Mede quietly. Stan did not respond.

Mede then pecked at the wound. Stan flinched and let out a quiet whimper but didn't move. Mede pecked and pecked until a small drop of yellow goo oozed out, followed by a strange, molten, dark shape. It looked like a raindrop made of dark mercury. Jack realised it had similarities to the Dark Rain.

"What is it?" asked Jack.

Mede didn't answer; he was too focused, carefully carrying the droplet in his beak. He flew to the fire, ceremoniously dropping it into the flames, where it burst into multicoloured sparks, like a mini firework.

"What was that?" asked Jack.

"That was the energy changing. The fire turns it from a negative to positive and frees it to be sparks of light. Fire can be very transformational. If the drop had burst inside of Stan, it carries pure nothingness and would have killed him," said Mede calmly, his eyes still fixed on Stan.

Jack reached down and stroked Stan's head, breathing gently onto his forehead and stroking his nose.

"Mia, remember the gift from hornbeam? The leaves, they will help the wound," said Mede.

Mia reached into the pack and found the leaves. She took her knife and used the handle to crush the leaves, remembering what she had seen Snakeskin do, and then she laid them carefully on Stan's open wound. Stan's eyelids flickered, and he started to wriggle his legs.

"Stan, Stan!" said Jack.

Mia and Jack continued to stroke him, as he started to come around. Mia let out a heavy exhale.

"Jack, I was so afraid. I couldn't find you or see you. I didn't know what happened." Her voice was anxious and breathy. "You just vanished into the earth, into that hole. It was so deep, and you didn't answer me. I thought you were dead," she said quietly.

Jack looked up, and they held each other's gaze for a moment. Mia then turned away, in slight embarrassment, tears silently sliding down her face.

"Is he going to be OK?" she asked.

"I hope so. I think we were just in time," said Mede, "but Stan needs to rest."

They sat in silence for a moment. Mia was still holding her knife, turning it in her hands, looking at the symbols. She traced her finger around the largest symbol; it was like a wonky H.

"What do we do now?" asked Mia. "Where are we? How do we get to the others?" Her voice was tense and tired.

Ayah spoke from her perch in the hawthorn tree's branches. "I will fly up and see if I can see them," she said and took to the wing.

Mede sat by Stan's head, whispering into his ear. Jack could not make out the words, but they sounded foreign, or magic. Suddenly, Stan's tail flopped up and down, beating the ground slowly, a very lazy tail wag. His eyes were not open yet, but Jack shrieked with joy. "Stan, you're awake!" he yelled.

One dog-eye opened, and then the other, and Stan's little mouth curled into a small, but familiar, toothy grin. They laughed and whooped with joy. Jack embraced his dog, tears pouring down his dirty cheeks. He held him close.

"Stan, you can't leave me ever," Jack whispered into his ear. Then he turned to Mede, wiping away his tears. "Mede, thank you, thank you," he said quietly.

Ayah swooped down through the gap in the trees. "I found them! They are not far for me flying, but they are across the great fracture, and it is a long way around by foot," she said.

A distant wolf's howl cut through the air. Jack's heart leapt hearing Wolf. He wished they were all together, right now, but he was tired to his bones.

"I don't think I can go on just now, and Stan is weak. I think we might need to make camp here for tonight," said Jack.

Stan lifted his head and gave Jack a lick on his hand in agreement. Jack smiled and rubbed his dog's head.

"Jack is right," said Mede, looking around the group.

Jack glanced over to the badgers, who had been lying quietly to one side. "Could we stay here with you tonight?" he asked.

The badgers raised their heads. Steel spoke: "Of course, you are all welcome. I do not think we want to go back to our underground den; that is a little too small for us all."

"No, I don't think I can go there again," said Jack, "no offence."

"You can make a camp under my branches," came the soft voice of the hawthorn tree. "I will cast protection around us."

"I would like that," said Mia quietly.

"We can keep watch too," said the badger.

"Snakeskin said we must be vigilant – the cracks and a Breaking could appear at any time. We must get to them as soon as we can in the morning," said Ayah.

Hearing that, Jack's stomach clenched, but he knew he was too tired to go on. He curled up next to Stan. Mia lay down the other side of Stan, quiet in her own thoughts. Mede and Ayah perched in the hawthorn tree above them, and Steel and Grey, the badgers, lay either side of them. Doubt started to creep into Jack's mind, doubt that he could be of any help, do anything at all to stop the terrible destruction of the natural world and do anything to stop The Forgetting, the ancient soul of the earth, destroying everything.

Chapter 8

The morning dawned with a strange orange hue to the light; the breeze was still strong, rattling the overhead branches, carrying the whispered call from the trees.

"You must go – you must get to the Lock."

The two badgers' cold noses nudged at Jack and Mia. "It's dawn," they said together.

Jack opened his eyes, grasping at the last wisps of a dream he had been having, a dream about a shimmering, beautiful fire creature flying through an ancient wood. He rubbed his sleepy eyes and looked at Stan, who was awake but still curled up in a small ball, not bouncing around in his usual way. Jack stretched his stiff and cold limbs, realising his T-shirt was still caked in mud from pulling Stan through the tunnel. He laid his hand on Stan.

"Are you OK?" he asked quietly.

"I'm OK, just a little weak," said Stan, not very convincingly.

"He needs some of Snakeskin's stronger medicine and food, but all will be well," said Mede.

Jack was glad of the wise bird's company. He turned to the badgers, who were standing quietly. "Thank you, thank you," Jack said, and stroked their heads.

"You are welcome, Jack," they said together.

"I'll carry you," said Jack, picking up his dog.

"It's this way," said Ayah, flying up and over where many trees had fallen the day before. The hawk found flying easier in the open space. And so, Jack and Mia began their journey to find the others, zigzagging and clambering over and around the upturned roots. Jack held tight to Stan.

"I am so hungry," said Jack.

"Me too," said Mia. "We've got those beech nuts Aster gave us," she said, rummaging in her rucksack.

"Good idea, kind of," said Jack with a smile.

They walked on, with Mia trying to feed Jack the beech nuts, as his hands were full carrying Stan. Stan kept pushing up his nose and pretending to try and eat them before they got to Jack's mouth, making them laugh. A warmth flowed through Jack seeing Stan regain some of his cheekiness.

Ayah swooped down. "We must follow the line of pine trees. They will take us to a stream at the bottom of the hill," she said.

"Water," said Stan.

"Oh, I am so thirsty," said Mia.

"Me too," said Jack.

They bumbled down the hill as fast as they could, with Stan jiggling in Jack's arms. Collapsing by the stream, they took huge gulps of the cool water from their cupped hands. Stan lapped at the water slowly, life flowing back to his small body. Jack washed the wound on Stan's leg and then laid some more of the hornbeam leaves on it. Stan turned and licked Jack's face, who laughed and hugged his dog.

"We cannot stop," called Ayah, "we have to move on now!"

"OK! Come on then, let's find them!" Jack shouted with a new-found positivity.

They set off across the stream, clambering up through the pine wood. Under the dark pine trees there was less undergrowth; the going was easier, and they could walk faster.

"You're nearly there," came the voice of a large pine tree ahead of them. "Keep going. You have to go around the rock at the top of the hill and then follow the line of ash trees. Ayah will meet you ahead – the trees are too dense for her to fly with you."

"Thank you," called Jack as they walked on past.

Stan looked up at his friend. "Thank you," he said to Jack. His dark eyes were brimming with love.

"Stop it," said Jack, half laughing. "I was so worried. You are going to be OK now, aren't you?" said Jack.

"I think so, thanks to you," said Stan, "but I do need a wee!"

"Oh great! I'll put you down then. Can you stand up?"

Jack carefully stood Stan on the ground, but Stan wobbled a lot when he tried to cock his leg, making an *ahwoahwooo* kind of a noise. Mia and Jack laughed out loud.

"OK, I don't think I'm ready for walking just yet," said Stan.

"That's convenient." Jack laughed sarcastically. "You know how much I love carrying you." Stan was heavy, and Jack's legs were tiring, but he didn't want to voice it. "Are the howls getting closer or am I imagining that?" he asked Mia.

"I'm not really sure; it's quite confusing. I think closer," she answered.

"All I keep thinking about is eating a big breakfast of fried eggs and toast and jam."

"Don't!" Mia laughed. "I would love some toast and jam right now. Or pancakes with maple syrup."

"Oh yes!" shouted Jack.

A loud wolf howl stopped their daydreams. Above them, Ayah let out a piercing cry, and Mede squawked. There was a *whoop* and Aster came tearing out of the trees towards them. "We've found them!" she yelled out. Other voices called out from the trees. "Are you OK? It was awful; we just couldn't get to you. How did you get out? What happened?" Aster's words were tumbling out. "We were so worried."

To Mia's obvious surprise, Aster pulled her into a big hug, then turned and tried to hug Jack and Stan together. They all laughed.

"Oh, Stan, are you OK?" said Aster, and both girls started fussing over him.

Jack started to tell them about the badgers and the hole and the hawthorn tree, when Snakeskin appeared out of the woods, smiling her broad smile. "We are so relieved to see you all. Mede has told me about Stan. Jack, would you lay him down so I can see him? What happened exactly?" she asked.

"The Forgetting's poison, I got it out just in time, but he is terribly weak," said Mede.

"It felt like my blood was burning," said Stan.

Snakeskin started touching around the wound on Stan's leg gently with her fingers and dropped her special tincture into his mouth. She looked into his eyes, lifting his eyelids. "Jack, Mede, you did well. I believe Stan will be well," she said, "but we have to move on; we cannot stop here."

"I will carry him if you like," said Aster.

"Oh, thank you! I won't say no," said Jack. "What happened back there?"

Lela spoke up. "That was a Breaking, when The Forgetting energy ruptures out of the earth. She is flowing deeper and deeper into the Root Network. We need to find a way to change it before it is too late," she hissed.

"But what is this being?" asked Mia.

"She is old and ancient, from the dawn of time, she was the holder of the balance. At first, she wanted to take away the pain of the destruction of nature, but there was too much, and she started to grow into it; the sadness and dark force became her. Now it is as if she wants to suck everything back to a void of nothing, like a black hole. We must restore the balance, her balance, to stop the destruction," said Lela.

Chapter 9

They entered a clearing ringed by flowering hawthorn trees; the white petals were blowing like confetti on the wind, it felt so different to where they had just been. To one side of the clearing was a huge fallen birch tree; its old, white bark was peeling, and its roots stuck up like bent fingers. Jack slumped down, and Aster lay Stan next to him on her shawl. Jack reached out and laid his hand on Stan's back; relief flowed through him – he was so happy they were all back together.

"We are at the Lock. Gebo the Birch, one of our Tree Elders, once stood here and she, with the help of the Earth Elders, helped to weave this Lock. She then fell, to create a gateway to the Lock and to the inner path, through to the land beyond. It is her greatest gift." She paused for a moment and started walking around as if she were looking for something. "Our village clan will have moved through here some days ago," she said. "I hope they were OK and did not get caught in the fractures. Lela, would you have seen that?" she asked.

“I believe I still would. I do not feel that death was here,” hissed Lela gently.

“And going through this will take us to a different land and time?” asked Jack, sitting up.

“Yes,” said Snakeskin, “but we must work out how to open the Lock. As Lela told you, it is protected, and will only open in times of extreme need. It is too dangerous for it to be open to anyone or anything; it would upset the balance. The Elders who protect this Lock have created a kind of code, to make sure only the right people can get through, and it changes depending on who is entering. You must prove yourself to the Lock or the path will not be clear,” said Snakeskin.

“Why can’t you help us?” asked Mia.

“The Locks vary for everyone. They are not set; they are ever-changing.”

“Even now when it is so important?” asked Jack.

“Yes, it is to protect us all. It will be something that you know or can work out. It takes great effort to move through the Lock. You will be tested. We will be close to the bedrock, and the pull of the deep earth is strong. After all you have been through, your energies are too weak to go through today; we will have to camp here tonight so you can rest.”

“Help me build a shelter,” said Aster, as she wandered around collecting sticks and bracken. Jack and Mia wearily started to help her.

Hearing singing, Jack turned and saw that Snakeskin was carefully tending to the branches and twigs from the bundle she carried. She was singing quietly, touching each stick gently and pouring water onto them from her water pouch; Wolf was at her side. Jack watched quietly, intrigued. Once she had finished with the sticks, she started to tend to Stan's wound, taking herbs from the pouch around her neck, delicately dabbing the swollen and red flesh. Stan was lying quietly with his eyes open. Jack saw her frown and whisper to Lela; he listened hard.

"I wish I felt safe here, but I do not. I had hoped we could go through tonight, but I fear for Stan; something does not seem right," she said.

The snake nodded her head slowly. Jack's stomach tightened.

Ayah and Mede sat perched on a branch above Jack. Ayah suddenly spoke so that Jack, to his initial annoyance, could no longer hear Snakeskin. "Mia, you show great courage staying for the journey. If you will allow me to, I would like to come with you," she said. "My wing has healed, and my far sight can help to guide you, especially on the plains. I offer myself as your guide."

Mia looked at the hawk and then Jack. "Thank you, Ayah, I would like that." Mia managed a small smile. The beauty of the bird and her piercing stare was awe-inspiring. Ayah flew and settled on her shoulder for a moment.

"I will fly above, keeping a lookout. If you need me then whistle or call. I will hear you and dive down. Can you whistle?" Ayah asked.

Mia looked down, biting her lip.

"Do you want to try?" Ayah asked.

Embarrassment spread across Mia's face; she nodded slowly in response. Ayah took off and flew up into the sky above the clearing. Mia reluctantly tried whistling, but the sound was too quiet to be heard above the wind and creaking trees. She glanced at Jack. "This is stupid," she said.

"It's OK, go for it," he whispered.

Mia looked at Jack, a cold stare, but Stan joined in from his sick bed. "Mia, try it. Listen, I can whistle," said Stan. He started making farting, spluttering noises. Mia looked at the dog and managed a strained laugh. "I'm not sure what you think is funny," said Stan, grinning.

After a moment, they all started whistling and laughing; only Aster was any good.

"I've always wanted to know how to properly whistle," said Mia, putting her thumb and index finger in her mouth and pursing her lips around them. She made a loud raspberry sound. "This just doesn't work," she said, grumpily.

"Well, I hope Ayah hears you, or this is going to get very confusing if you all start whistling – you'll have me running every which way!" said Stan with mock seriousness.

They all laughed, but Jack was not convinced by Stan's upbeat tone. He thought his voice sounded thin and weak.

"Why don't you just sing a high note," said Aster, "it is how I call the wolves." She let out a loud, piercing note. Jack saw Wolf raise her head.

Mia pushed away her embarrassment, lifted her head and sung a high-pitched sound. It was a plaintive note, loud and clear, and the more she sang, the stronger it got. Ayah came swooping down and landed on her shoulder. Everyone cheered, and Jack saw Mia grin. He didn't say anything, but he knew how magical it was to connect with an animal like that.

"We must study the Lock before it gets dark," said Mede with authority.

Jack peered into the dark, gnarled crevice. At first, all Jack could see was old roots, stones and dried earth, but as his eyes adjusted, he saw a small, narrow, moss-covered door, right at the centre of the cavity. He squatted down to get a better look. Mia walked to Jack – she had a new confidence, Ayah on her shoulder. Mede was perched above them with his head on one side, studying the entrance. There were intricate and delicate symbols carved into the door; Jack reached out to touch them. "What are those?" Jack asked, pointing.

"The ancient code that we need to understand to work out how to open the door," said Mede. "Remember them – let your mind work on what they might mean."

"Look at that symbol," Mia said. "It's like a spiral. It looks familiar, like I've seen it somewhere before."

Jack turned to the door and traced his fingers over the markings; he noticed that there were also two slots cut into the wood either side of the symbols. He held his fingers over the slots.

"That symbol there, the one like two triangles on its side, is that infinity?" she asked.

"I'm not sure, maybe," said Jack.

Aster walked over to join them; she too had never seen or been through the Lock. They started touching the symbols and marks on the door.

"Do you know what those mean?" asked Jack.

"Those are the symbols of The Runes. We use them for divination. The one like a sideways triangle means fire or awakening, and the X is Gebo, which means sacrifice or divine interaction."

"Wasn't the Tree Elder, the tree that made the Lock, called Gebo?" asked Jack.

"Yes," said Aster.

"And what is the last symbol? The one like the wonky H?" Mia asked.

"That is Hegalaz. It represents air, and transformation," said Aster.

"How does any of this show us how are we meant to open the door?" asked Mia, seeming to like the puzzle.

"You have to work it out," said Mede.

Snakeskin's call interrupted their thoughts. "The dark is descending, come, we must eat and then rest."

She handed them some grey-looking bread-like stuff – it was hard and chewy but with a nutty taste. They ate in silence. It was not the tasty meal Jack had dreamed of; his tummy rumbled loudly.

"We must be ready to move through the Lock at first light," she said. "The fractures and a Breaking could begin at any moment. Come to the shelter and rest." Her voice was controlled.

Jack sensed she was attempting to appear calm but

was anything but. They all lay in a long line, Snakeskin and Lela on the outside; Stan was curled up between Jack and Mia. The birds perched high in the nearby trees, and Wolf lay in front of them, watching. Night fell quickly, blanketing them all in velvety darkness. Jack was tired, but sleep did not come easily. The events of the day kept running through his mind. All around them, the forest made strange, creaking noises, but the night creatures seemed eerily silent. He tried shutting his eyes but kept opening them to check on Stan and Mia. He felt bad that Mia was with him, he hadn't intended to bring her, but now he was *actually* glad of her company. He heard whispering, and realised it was Snakeskin and Lela talking quietly.

"My friend, how I fear what is coming. I hope I have the strength to complete the task at hand. I will miss you," said Snakeskin, her voice sad.

"You know it will be like a birth. You will find the strength. I would not have chosen you otherwise. Efil will help us both," came the low hiss of Lela.

He opened his eyes and Mia was staring at him, her eyes wide open too.

"Jack," she whispered, "what are they saying? I'm scared." There was a softness to her voice, not something Jack had really heard before.

"I don't know. I'm scared too," said Jack.

"Do you think Stan will be OK?" she asked.

"I'm OK," said Stan. "It doesn't hurt so much now."

"You need to rest," said Jack quietly.

Mia reached out. "Jack, I'm afraid – can I hold your hand?" she whispered.

Jack reached out and took her hand. It felt a bit awkward at first, but it was reassuring, and he needed that just now.

"Tom is going to be so cross I'm doing this," Mia said quietly. "He'll hate it. I'm not allowed to do anything without him normally. It's a twin thing. I'm more scared of him than I am of my parents."

"Why do you let him treat you like that?" asked Jack.

"It's just how it has always been. I do what he says. He was the firstborn, and apparently when you are twins that makes him better than me. He's very persuasive, you know."

"Yep, I know," Jack mumbled.

"My parents never believe me; they're always on his side," she whispered.

"Oh, I see." Jack's voice sounded hollow. He paused for a moment. "So, you took it out on me?"

"I'm sorry. You have no idea what it's like. It's OK for you on your own. I dream of that sometimes."

"You wouldn't like it," said Jack.

"I am going to be in so much trouble – you have no idea," said Mia dejectedly.

"Well, yesterday time seemed to pass differently here than at home. I spent a long time here, but when I went back, I was home by the end of the day. I'm going to be in trouble too. I keep going off. I suppose there's nothing we can do. Let's not think about it," he said.

Mia turned away. "This is a mess," she said. "It was bad enough before the house was flooded, but this is going to be a disaster. I'll be grounded forever."

"There's no point thinking about it. Let's worry about being grounded later," said Jack, rather unconvincingly.

Mia mumbled something Jack didn't hear. They lay in silence, still holding hands, and his frustration with Mia passed. So much had changed; it was strange that what had happened in the past didn't seem important right now. Mia seemed to be asleep, but then suddenly she spoke. "Jack, those symbols, the spirals! They are the same as the ones on my knife. I can't believe I didn't realise before. Maybe yours has them too? Quick, look. Does your torch work?"

Jack fumbled in his pocket and pulled out his torch. It gave out a weak light, but just enough to see that the knife did have symbols carved into it. Jack traced his fingers down the handle – yes of course, there was the spiral and the X, just as they had seen them on the door, only much smaller.

"Jack, look! Mine has the infinity one. Maybe our knives are like some kind of key!" she said.

"Yes! You're brilliant, Mia," said Jack. A wave of relief went through his mind.

Jack looked back at Mia, but she had shut her eyes and seemed to have already gone to sleep – had she been talking in her sleep? He switched off the torch and shut his eyes too, but instead of sleep, his mind started turning over question after question about things he had seen and heard that day. What was Snakeskin doing with the sticks? What were Snakeskin and Lela talking about? Who was Efil? Finally, he fell into a fitful, dream-filled sleep.

Chapter 10

Jack was deep in a dream, when suddenly, Snakeskin was shaking them all awake. For a moment, he didn't know where he was – it was still a penetrating dark.

"We must go, now! The Breakings are coming again. Lela has foreseen it."

"But it's dark – how will we work out how to get through the Lock?" asked Jack nervously, trying to shake off sleep. "And what about Stan? Is he well enough?"

"We have to go," Snakeskin repeated. "Stan, you are going to have to be strong. We have no choice. We must move *now*!"

Mia seemed to jolt awake. She jumped up and pushed her way out of the shelter; Jack saw she had her knife in her hand.

"Jack, get your knife," she shouted out behind her.

Wolf was standing ready outside the shelter, and Mede and Ayah were perched on the upturned roots. There was a shuddering through the earth below their feet and a wind was picking up. Jack ran to the door holding his torch; its dim light just lit the markings on the door. Mia traced her fingers along the spirals and then the two slits in the wood. She poked at it with her knife; it slipped into the slot perfectly.

"Jack, my knife fits in the hole, quick, try yours," she said.

Hurriedly, he pushed his knife into the other hole between the symbols. "They fit!" he shouted.

All the symbols started to glow as Jack had seen them do when he was in the badger hole, and the Lock started to judder and creak. They pushed at the door, but it didn't open.

"It's not working, what now?" shouted Jack. "What have we done wrong?"

Mia pushed and pushed at it. "What about that other symbol? That one, the one that's not on the knives," she said, pointing.

"Maybe we have to do something else?" Jack was starting to panic.

A huge cracking sound boomed from the wood around them. Aster came running up behind them. "It means air!" shouted Aster and Snakeskin almost simultaneously.

"What do we do about air?" shouted Mia, her voice frantic.

"Breathe on the door maybe," Aster shouted.

They all crowded around the door: Jack, Mia, Aster, Snakeskin, Stan, Lela, Wolf, with Mede and Ayah perched in the branches above.

"Quickly, blow," shouted Aster. "Now!"

They all blew hard on the door. There was a sudden high ringing sound.

"Yes!" cawed Mede.

"Push now!" hissed Lela.

They pushed and the door made a shrill noise and opened to reveal a tunnel ahead of them. The earth around them shuddered. Wolf darted through the door, and they scrambled in after her.

"Stan!" shouted Jack over his shoulder.

"Yes. I'm coming," he called back.

"Aster! Quickly, close the door!" Snakeskin called.

Inside the tunnel, they were greeted by a fierce, bright light, glaring like sun bouncing off a mirror. They stood shading their eyes and adjusting to the light. Surrounding them were shining, clear crystals glinting with rainbow colours.

"Wow, what is it?" asked Mia. "It's like a wall of diamonds."

"It reminds me of the crystal my mum has at home. I think maybe it's quartz," said Jack.

"Yes, ancient, powerful, clear and strong," said Snakeskin.

Aster reached out to steady herself. "Ow, it's sharp," she said.

"Stan, are you OK? Is it OK on your paws?" Jack called out.

"I'm OK," said Stan quietly. But Jack could see that Stan was not walking in his usual way.

"I'll carry you if you need it," said Jack.

"No, stop fussing," said Stan, "look, not wobbly."

Jack eyed his dog with concerned suspicion.

They started to walk up the crystal ravine, Wolf in the lead, followed by Snakeskin and Lela and then the kids with the birds on their shoulders. Stan followed at the back. The colours were magical, bouncing light all around them. The path was narrow and awkward, meaning they had to walk slowly and carefully. It was eerily quiet, no wind, no talking plants, but Jack felt like the ravine was watching and listening to them.

After they had walked for a while, Jack felt a strange feeling, like he was very tired, and the path seemed to be shimmering with a kind of dark, misty cloud. Snakeskin's voice suddenly rang out: "You must focus and be strong. We are nearing the deep centre, where the rocks emit a powerful force. It will pull you down if you are not careful. We cannot stop. Whatever happens, we *must* keep moving and cross over to the land of the plains. This will take all your strength! On no account should you stop – focus on the light from the crystals. Focus on seeing your way to the end of the tunnel. The air will be thin; it will feel like being up a mountain."

"I've not been up a mountain," mumbled Jack.

It was not long before Jack's legs started to feel leaden, as if they were being pulled down by thick mud, the sort that pulls your wellies off. Their pace slowed. Mia stumbled ahead of him. Jack looked around every so often to check on Stan, who seemed to jump to attention and wag his tail each time Jack looked at him, but Jack's instinct was getting stronger – something was not right.

Suddenly, Jack heard a weird noise, a muffled cry. He looked back, and Stan was on his side, writhing, his eyes rolling.

"I can't stand," gurgled Stan.

"Stan! Snakeskin! Help!" Jack screamed.

Snakeskin, who was up ahead, stopped in her tracks and turned to look. Jack had stopped, but now his legs felt like they were flowing into the rock below him, like he was held down by a mighty magnet.

"Oh, oh, help me," he said quietly, as he stood, wobbling back and forth.

He felt dizzy, the intensity of the force pulling at him was like nothing he had ever experienced before.

"Jack, pick up Stan!" yelled Snakeskin. "Keep focused on the crystals and the light. Everyone else, keep walking!"

Jack started to feel as if he just wanted to slide down the walls and lie down; his movements became slower and slower. Snakeskin scrambled back to him, while trying to make her shawl into a kind of sling. Once she got to Jack, she tied it around him, like a baby carrier, and then she and Jack stood swaying while struggling to tie Stan on. It took an enormous effort, but finally they managed it, Stan's head poked over the top, but his head kept lolling and his eyes rolling. Snakeskin pushed Jack forward. "Walk! Come on, Jack!" she shouted while gently shoving Jack forward.

He stood, wavering back and forth. He felt like he couldn't move. "I can't," he mumbled.

"You have to!" she shouted, her voice kind but firm, gently pushing him forward again.

Jack focused hard on the crystals above him and the girls in front of him and forced one leg to move. Slowly, one step after another, he started to wade through the heavy energy. It was like walking in deep water, each step an effort.

Mia then suddenly tripped. Aster quickly turned and grabbed her, pulling her along.

"Come on!" Aster shouted.

"Jack, we must keep moving – all our lives depend on it, especially Stan's. We must get through the ravine – *walk*!" Snakeskin roared.

Mia turned to reach for Jack's hand, and he stretched to grasp Mia's. As he did, he looked down, and his eye was drawn to a beautiful shard of crystal at his feet. It really glistened in the light. Staggering, he managed to reach down and grab it, while being propelled forward by Mia. At that moment, a strange, clear note started, like the single note on a violin, soft and harmonious.

"That is a message!" said Snakeskin with an upbeat tone. "It is the crystals' healing song – they must see your strength. The crystal has been offered to you, as a healing gift for Stan," she said.

Jack held the crystal tight in his palm. The group walked, snaking their way along, like an infant school party, their spirits lifted by the music. Stan poked his head up from inside his carry-sling, his eyes open and his little lip curled up in a smile.

"I could get used to this," he said quietly.

Hearing his dog, Jack grinned. The heaviness started to lift, and walking became easier. The ravine turned into something more like a tunnel, dimmer and wider, and the crystals were replaced by dark granite rock. They walked on, feeling their way along the damp walls. In the distance, Jack could see a glow of light. Wolf turned and looked at Snakeskin, who nodded, and Wolf loped ahead. Ayah took to the air and flew out of the tunnel, desperate to fly high again.

Finally, they all stumbled through a gap between some huge boulders, out into the light. Jack stood gulping the fresh air, squinting in the sun. Ahead of them were plains for as far as the eye could see, so different to the tunnel and the woods they had left behind. Tall, yellowy grasses were blowing in the light breeze. There was no storm here, no upturned trees, no tree stumps, just miles of wild grassland. It felt like an early summer's day, almost perfect. A small stream was trickling amongst the rocks; they plunged their hands in, drinking handfuls and handfuls of the cool water. Jack felt it reviving him from the inside.

"We made it," said Snakeskin, "but quickly, we must tend to Stan. Light a small fire. Mede, come," she said.

Aster lifted Stan out of the sling on Jack's back and laid him on the ground. Jack sat beside Stan and took his head onto his lap, stroking his tufty hair. Stan just lay there, hardly moving. The others set about making a fire. Mia came over, carrying a water pouch. Jack slowly dripped some water into Stan's mouth. Mede perched on Stan's back leg.

"Sorry," he said quietly, "I think there might still be poison – I need to look again. It may hurt."

Mede started gently pecking at the wound. Snakeskin knelt beside him, and as Mede pecked, she pressed around the wound. Stan flinched. Mede pecked and pecked, while Snakeskin pushed at the edge of the wound while she chanted some words. They worked quietly, without fuss. Stan's face looked strained.

"I have to make a small cut," said Snakeskin, carefully cutting the wound a little. Stan made a quiet yip sound as a large, orangey globule of pus oozed out of the wound. Within it was a dark shape, another large, mercury-like raindrop. It rolled around without breaking. Snakeskin took a sharp intake of breath.

"The poison was deep, the nothingness spreading," she whispered. "We do not want that to escape here, in this land, we must be rid of it quickly."

Mede carefully picked up the droplet in his beak and flew to the fire. Again, he ceremoniously dropped it into the centre of the flames. Just as before, as it hit the flames, it burst into multicoloured sparks, but these were bigger and redder than the last.

"The poison was strong," said Snakeskin, "but, Stan, you were stronger – you did well not to succumb to the power of it. I hope and believe that is the last drop – you will heal fast now."

Snakeskin washed the cut and then laid herbs of willow

bark and hornbeam leaves on it. Jack pulled the crystal he had found out of his pocket and laid it on the top. Stan started moving, and his eyes flickered open. Jack held Stan in his arms, relief flowing through him; he couldn't lose Stan.

"More stroking, I need more," said Stan.

Everyone laughed. The girls came over and they started fussing and stroking him.

"This feels like a good place to rest before we cross the plain," said Snakeskin. "We have some cover and protection from the rocks for tonight."

Jack saw Lela slither off Snakeskin's arm and disappear under one of the boulders, no doubt in search of peace and cool darkness. But something was weird – she seemed to be shimmering like a heat haze. Jack double-blinked and she looked normal again. *A trick of the light*, he thought.

Ayah was hovering high in the sky, surveying the surroundings; her acute eyesight better suited this open grassland. Below her, Wolf howled, and from somewhere out in the tall grass, another howl answered. Jack watched Wolf – her body had become alert and taut, as she stood staring out across the plains.

"Do you ever have to fight other wolf packs?" he asked. He had watched and read enough to know wolves were territorial.

"It's OK, this is the land of my old family. I left to protect the village and Snakeskin, but I am always welcome here. All is well." She turned away and quietly loped off into the long grass, her back and tail swinging as she moved. Jack watched the grasses sway as she disappeared out of view.

Looking for his torch, Jack started delving through the side pockets of his trousers. His fingers touched on a rustling packet and, with a "whoop", Jack pulled out a very, very crushed packet of crisps.

"Mia, look!" he said, holding up the crisp packet. "I forgot I had these!"

He pulled open the packet and they each reached in. Aster cautiously nibbled at one, wrinkling her nose.

"Those are weird," she said, laughing.

"They taste pretty good to me," said Jack. Something other than beech nuts was a treat. They sat for a moment, savouring the crushed, salty crisps.

"Aster," asked Jack tentatively, "what has happened to Sylvie?"

He had thought of Sylvie often on the journey. Aster looked down and paused for a moment.

"She went ahead to the gathering with the clan, so I don't know really." She bit her lip. "She was already changing."

"Oh, I'm sorry," he said quietly. "I hope we can help."

"Yes, so do I."

She turned her head away; Jack could feel her sadness. They sat in silence.

The sun was starting to set when Ayah and Wolf returned. Wolf carried meat in her jaws; she laid it at Snakeskin's feet. "Thank you," said Snakeskin, as she touched Wolf's nose with her own. Snakeskin sat by the fire preparing a meal from the meat, wild garlic and nettles she had picked along the way, along with some nuts and berries from her stores. She also handed out some more of the hard acorn bread – it was chewy and dry, but its nutty taste was OK. Even Mia did not complain and ate everything. Jack quietly watched Stan gnawing some meat off a bone. As darkness fell, they settled down for the night. Mede perched in a bush by the rocks and the animals took turns to keep watch. In the quiet, Mia tuned to Jack.

"I miss home."

"Yeah, me too. My mum will be so worried and alone."

"Where's your dad?" she asked.

"Uh…" Jack looked away. An awkward silence followed.

"Oh, sorry, I didn't mean to, um, pry or anything. I had thought your parents were divorced. I don't know, but you've said some things," said Mia, suddenly embarrassed at having asked.

"It's OK – you didn't know," said Jack. He took a deep breath in and then added, "My dad died."

"Oh," said Mia. "I'm so sorry," she said quietly.

"It's not been a great year," said Jack.

"Oh, I really am sorry. And I'm so sorry we, um, treated you the way we did. I'm sorry," said Mia meekly.

"It's over now, right?" said Jack.

"Yep, it's definitely over. I just have to learn to stand up to Tom now," she said.

"Yes!" said Jack.

They both fell silent. Jack shut his eyes, glad of Stan's warm body next to him, his mind drifting back to his dad.

Jack awoke with the blissful feeling of the heat of the morning sun on his back. He rolled over to see Snakeskin talking to Ayah and Wolf by the fire. Stan was sitting with them, looking Alert. Mia caught Jack's eye and smiled. He jumped up and ran to Stan, flinging his arms around his dog.

"You are OK!" he said.

Stan did a funny dog twirl. "I'm much better, and I'm very hungry," he said.

Wolf dragged some meat to Stan which he devoured ravenously. Snakeskin passed around more of the cooked meat too. It was delicious – they all relished it – Jack licked his fingers repeatedly for every last morsel; he looked to Wolf and nodded a thank you. Gazing out over the plains, Jack felt so free – there was miles of wide-open space. In the far distance, he could see what looked like a white hill.

"Today, we must cross the plains to the river near the hills, into the Pando, to meet 'Eye' our Great Elder," said Snakeskin. "There, the clans are preparing for the Great Fire Gathering. It may feel quiet now, but The Forgetting is still penetrating the Rings and with her comes the impending storm. We know we have to be ready – there is no second chance – we must move on," Snakeskin said.

Lela slithered out from under the rocks, up Snakeskin's arm and around her neck. Her eyes were burning with their usual fire, but also reflected the white of the far-off hills. Jack saw her shimmer, again. He rubbed his eyes and she looked normal again. Lela was unusually quiet though, and Jack kept thinking about the conversation he had overheard between Snakeskin and Lela before they entered the Lock, and about their task. It had sounded so serious.

"How come it's so wild and no one is here?"

"It is a different Ring of Time. This place has stayed untouched, thankfully, it is why we chose it; the natural energy here still has life force," said Snakeskin.

"I will carry Stan," said Aster, "while he regains his strength."

They set off, Stan's nose poking out from the sling on Aster's back.

"Don't get used to this," said Jack, laughing.

"I'll try not to." He grinned. "I could try singing if you like," he said.

"No!" came the shout in unison. Everyone started laughing.

"You will be walking soon if you start singing, Stan," said Jack.

Jack felt so alive walking out in the open with the gentle breeze on his face; it was hard to comprehend there was any kind of threat at all.

Chapter 11

The sun was now high in the sky; the heat pulsed around them; and walking had become gruelling. Mia's face was fixed with a determined expression; sweat was trickling down her forehead. Aster had her head down and trudged along. The white hills had not looked that far away from the camp, but it had been deceptive; they had been walking for what seemed like hours, but there was still a long way to go. Stan's whistling had kept up morale for a while, but now everyone was tired. Jack's mouth was dry with thirst, but the water supply was running low, and he knew he had to wait.

"We cannot rest," said Snakeskin, as if reading his mind, "it's too exposed here."

Lela suddenly put her head up; Jack followed her gaze. "What do you see?" he asked.

"Horses," whispered Lela.

Snakeskin stood still and surveyed the approaching horses. They all stopped, watched and waited. Jack could see from the dust in the air that the horses were travelling at speed, like in an old western film. One horse was galloping out in front with a rider on its back. Jack felt a nervous tingle run through his body.

The rider, a man with greying curly hair and a tattoo on his forehead, pulled up in front of them. He leapt from his horse and walked over to Wolf, who stood still out in front of the group. The man bent down and touched noses with Wolf, and then Snakeskin smiled her big smile and opened her arms. The man looked up and having shown respect to Wolf, he walked to Snakeskin and took her outstretched hands in his.

"Sister," he said. "At last." His voice was strong but kind. Jack let out a sigh – he had been expecting something bad, but he could see now that the man looked similar to Snakeskin, with a slightly hooked nose, and with the same tattoo in the shape of a spiral.

"We have been a long time preparing for this moment, waiting and praying you would make it through," the man said.

"It is so good to see you and to know that we are facing this together," said Snakeskin.

Aster ran and threw her arms around the man, burying her head in his shoulder.

"Hello, Little Otter," he said.

Aster let out a quiet sob and Jack turned away. He found it hard to see her vulnerable, she was usually so strong and capable; his heart thumped faster.

"I'm so afraid, Uncle, and so worried for Lela," she whispered.

"Lela knows the path she has chosen. You must not fear," he said, and then the man looked to Jack and Mia, and held out his hands towards them. "I am Blaine," he said.

"Hello, I'm Jack."

"I'm Mia."

Blaine then peered at the bundle on Aster's back and nodded at the little nose poking out.

Stan grinned. "I'm Stan."

"Well, welcome, Stan," said Blaine, smiling. "You are all very welcome here. We have wished and prayed for someone from your time to come, and you have answered us," said Blaine.

There was a distant rumble of thunder; the horse's ears twitched. Lela stared into the distance, her cool eyes looking out across the plain.

"We must go," she said with her slow, hissing voice.

Snakeskin and Blaine nodded. Wiping her face, Aster turned away from Blaine and walked straight to one of the horses. She stood whispering into its ear; the horse stood stock still, just bowing its head a little. Aster vaulted onto the horse with ease. Snakeskin lifted Stan up, so he could sit in front of Aster on the horse.

"He is not strong enough to walk this distance. Aster, he can ride with you," she said.

Stan had a funny expression. Jack couldn't tell if it was fear or relief. He watched him for a moment and couldn't help laughing at the sight of Stan riding in style. Blaine walked over and talked to one of the horses, a smallish, slightly round, grey mare.

"Jack, Mia, you are small enough to ride together, you may find it easier, and this is Mist – she is kind and comfortable. The horses are much quicker than we could hope to travel on foot, and time is running out. The Forgetting is pushing through, and the storm is coming. Mist will look after you and we will not travel too fast until you are ready," said Blaine.

"I'm not a very good rider," said Mia. "I've only ridden on holiday a few times, but that's it."

"Well, that is more than me," said Jack. "I've only ridden a bucking bronco machine at a fair!"

"Can I sit in front, so I can hold the mane?" asked Mia. "Then you can hold onto me."

With a lot of scrambling and flailing of legs, Blaine helped Jack and Mia onto the patient Mist. The fact that both him and Mia were here, sat on a horse together, struck Jack as being about as different as it could get from how things had been at home. Everything had changed so fast.

Snakeskin's horse held one leg up, and so Snakeskin used that to aid her vaulting onto her horse. They set off. Wolf set out in front with Blaine; Mede and Ayah were flying above them. The thunder was rumbling more frequently now, and far in the distance, the sky was a deep, threatening grey. Jack sensed that the birds were fearful and were staying closer to the group than would be normal. He knew that most birds would not usually fly during a storm.

At first, Jack and Mia kept nearly sliding off; they slipped all over the place and couldn't help giggling. Mia had quite good balance though and hung on tight to Mist's mane.

"I will take care of you," said Mist. "Try and relax and it will be easier."

Jack laughed. "Easier said than done, but I'll try."

He realised that talking to a horse now seemed to come naturally to him. Whenever Jack felt himself starting to slip, he felt Mist adjust her speed and stride as if to compensate. Slowly, he started to relax, letting her take control. After this, they both found it easier than expected and stopped bumping around quite so much. Jack reached into his pocket and pulled out the last of the beech nuts; they nibbled them as they rode. Not the best snack, but anything right now was welcome.

As they got better at riding, Jack and Mia rode alongside Aster, just behind Blaine and Snakeskin. Jack started to hear snippets of Snakeskin and Blaine's conversation. He heard enough to understand that Blaine normally lived in their village but had been away for some months preparing the Great Fire Gathering. He tried to get closer on Mist and strained to listen.

"I have visited as many of the Elders as I could, travelling far through different lands. On my return, Eye and I have spoken often. Animal scouts have taken word to the animal nations, and it has been good to see how many have come, and continue to arrive," said Blaine.

"I cannot tell you how good it is to see you, brother. It has been hard; everything has become so unbalanced. We were unsure if you were alive; even Lela couldn't see. It has felt very uncertain that we can fulfil our destiny," she said gently.

Listening to their conversation, Jack thought about Aster's reaction to Blaine – it made sense, if she had thought him dead, but he felt there was something else too, something about Lela. It disturbed him to see her so worried.

"When you were speaking to Blaine, what did you mean about being worried for Lela?" he asked.

"It's hard to explain," said Aster quietly.

"You seemed so, um, scared," said Jack.

"I am scared, but it is a secret we have kept for so long; Lela must tell you herself. It is her destiny to tell," said Aster, a finality in her voice, and she turned away.

Jack let it drop but didn't stop thinking about it as they rode on.

They covered much more ground on the horses than they had on foot, and from the higher vantage point, Jack could see that there were other animals following them. A herd of huge Bison and a wolf family pack were walking in parallel to them, a little way off in the long grass. Following them at a distance were the other horses from the herd Blaine had brought with him, as well as rabbits, deer, skunk, bears and badgers. It reminded him of images of *Noah's Ark*: a trail of animals coming through the long grasses. None of the usual rules of nature seemed to apply; they were all walking together peacefully.

"Aster, why are all the animals following us?"

“They are all heading to the Great Fire Gathering for the ceremony, travelling from different lands and some through the Lock like us. The Elders have worked hard to make this possible, opening channels that are normally closed, allowing for the greatest of gatherings. We will meet at a very sacred place, with Eye, our most revered Elder. He is one of the oldest living beings on earth and holds immense knowledge and wisdom. This is where the energy and life force are the strongest and so it is where we must face The Forgetting and the storm she brings,” she said.

Jack sensed Mia shudder. He put his hand on her shoulder, although he was not sure if he was calming himself or her. He felt far from home, exposed and vulnerable. How could they face such a being and such a storm? What could they do, sitting precariously on a horse? He felt a cold drip of sweat slide down his back.

Chapter 12

Tired, thirsty, and aching from riding a horse, they finally reached the river. The sun had begun to drop behind the trees. A cold wind was picking up; Jack shivered. Across the river, in the distance, he could see what looked like a silver-white forest, the white streak he had seen before from afar. The river was much bigger than he had expected – it was churning, and rough, white froth swirled on the surface.

"We must cross the river tonight," said Snakeskin firmly.

Jack saw Aster shoot Snakeskin a look. Blaine was already scouting the bank looking for the best place to cross. Jack saw him lean forward and speak to his horse. Mist seemed to be jittery beneath them; she did not stand still, and Jack sensed fear in the other horses too.

"Is the river safe?" asked Jack, looking at it uneasily.

"The soul of the earth is faltering, The Forgetting energy is already affecting everything, bringing the storm, the river is losing control," said Mist, "which is why we must cross now before it is too wild." Beneath him, Jack felt a nervous tremble ripple along Mist's body.

Blaine spoke up, his voice like a commanding officer. "We must stay together, and you must follow me. I know this river well; I will talk to her and she will help as best she can. Don't stray – follow in a line, and assist any of the other beings you can. It is important we all cross together, but quickly. The river spirit is crying, she knows she is out of control. Alder and Willow, standby. Otters, beavers, are you ready?"

Jack felt Mia's body tense up in front of him. A line of otters and beavers swum out into the river, each carrying a branch from the nearby willow and alder trees. They made a chain across the water, ready to catch anyone.

Mist turned her head to Jack and Mia, and said, "Hold on tight to my mane and each other."

Mia grabbed Mist's mane. Jack swallowed hard and held on tight to Mia's waist. Blaine's horse went first, then Jack and Mia, Aster with Stan, and Snakeskin with Lela last. They slid down the bank into the fast-flowing, white, frothy water, which came up to the top of Mist's belly. The cold water swirled around their legs, biting into their skin. They both gasped.

"Are you OK, Stan?" Jack called out behind him, but the sound of his voice was drowned out by the sounds of the river. Even with his fear, he smiled at how sweet Stan looked perched with Aster on their horse; it helped calm him a little. The other horses were crossing beside and behind them and Jack had never imagined he would see a rabbit or badger riding on the back of a horse, but that is exactly what was happening. For a moment, he wished he could have taken a photograph; no one would ever believe any of this. But within moments, they were in the pull of the strong current. Mist tripped and nearly unseated Jack.

"I'm sorry," she called.

"It's OK," said Jack, "it's much harder for you than us."

A loud crack of thunder made them all jump; even Mist, with her steady pace, twisted her spine. Mia gripped her mane. A young horse was struggling just ahead of them and Blaine's horse turned from the bank and whinnied a strong, low whinny. "Come herd, come."

The young horse lifted its head and kept on swimming, its legs straining in the strong current. A trail of animals were crossing the river too, landing exhausted on the opposite bank. Wolf was nearing the middle, where the water was most turbulent, paddling hard with the rest of the pack; her head was just above the water, and she had a strained look on her face. Jack noticed that Wolf's body was shielding the youngest members of the pack, who were making slow progress, and the current was so strong they were being carried downstream. Jack's eyes were fixed on Wolf, so he didn't see the large log floating towards them. Mia screamed too late, and the log hit Mist in the side. Mist fell, and both Jack and Mia were thrown off into the freezing and tempestuous river.

Blaine was on the bank watching and his scream

of, "*No!*" was carried on the wind. Jack and Mia found themselves hurtling towards the line of beavers and otters. Jack kept being pulled under, then he just managed to grab onto the tale of an otter in the line, but the tail was slippery and he let go. His head plunged under the water. He scrabbled and flailed his arms above his head and somehow managed to seize a willow branch and the smooth tail of another otter at the same time. He hung on with all his might, pulling his head just above the water line, casting his eyes for Mia, but as he did, he saw her disappear under the water and vanish from sight.

"Mia, Mia!" Jack spluttered. His heart was pounding. He looked over to Blaine who he could now see galloping down the riverbank on his horse. Mist was standing on the bank, her head down, breathing hard, looking utterly dejected. Jack kicked and kicked with all his strength to keep above water, clinging onto the willow-beaver line, unsure how to move on. With relief, he saw Aster and Stan make it to the bank. Suddenly, a hand was grabbing him, and Snakeskin had the back of his shirt. Her horse was breathing hard – the vapor from her nostrils came out in puffs of warmth right in his ear.

"Jack, hold on tight to Flint's mane, and I will hold onto you. We do not have far to go. We must get out of the river," her voice just audible over the rush of the water.

An otter broke from the chain and swam alongside Jack while he clung to the neck of Snakeskin's horse. Stumbling and slipping, her horse pulled itself up the slimy, muddy slope, out of the river and onto the bank. Jack fell onto the grass, breathing hard. Stan ran straight to him and licked his face.

"Are you OK? Are you OK?" panted Stan.

"Stan, we *have* to find Mia. You *have* to find Mia!" puffed Jack.

Without a word, Stan was off, running down the riverbank, following Blaine.

The trees were calling, and Jack could hear, "*Mia, Mia*," pass along the riverbank. Jack pulled himself up and set off staggering after Stan, breathing hard and coughing from the water he'd swallowed.

"Mia, Mia," he shouted as best he could, but his lungs had no strength.

He couldn't see any sign of the wolf pack either. The river seemed to be getting wilder: logs and debris were being flung here and there and Jack did not dare think about what could have happened. They had to find Mia. Up ahead, he saw the shape of Ayah battling the wind; her flying was erratic as she was buffeted around. Every so often, she stopped and hovered, as best she could, scanning the river with her acute eyesight. Jack became frantic – he screamed Mia's name, while Stan barked and called out from further down the bank. People were running out of the forest from the gathering to join them. Everyone was scouring the river. Voices rang out all around him.

Jack felt weak and drained and as if he had bricks for feet; he just couldn't run at speed. Where was she? A cold fear set into his body. Ahead, he could see a bend in the river, and a larger group of trees with Ayah hovering above. The trees had stopped calling Mia's name; instead, they were whispering, "*Alder, Alder, Alder the Protector, go to Alder the Protector.*" He saw Ayah swoop. At the same moment, he saw that some of the wolf pack were scrambling out of the river near the trees. Clawing their way up the roots in the bank, bedraggled and battered but alive. But where was Wolf? There was no sign of her or Mia. As he got closer, he saw that Blaine was with a group of other men and women, scrambling along the bank, scouring the water's edge. Stan was ahead of them, running up and down along the riverbank near the wolf pack, his nose to the ground. Mede was darting along the tree line and the trees were calling louder and louder, "*Alder the Protector.*" He saw Stan look up and bark something in the direction of Ayah who was hovering above him, but, in the wind, Jack could not hear what. Stan suddenly darted into the trees; Ayah swooped down; and Blaine began to run. Jack's heart leapt – it was like a switch went in his mind and life came back to his legs – he started running, as fast as he could.

"She's here!" cried Stan.

Jack arrived to see Mia's body lying caught between the branch and the roots of a giant alder tree, and to his surprise and relief, Wolf was standing in the muddy water beside her, very gently holding Mia's head out of the water by the back of her neck. The alder tree's branch was like an arm holding her up. Wolf was shaking all over from the exertion, but she did not let go, not until Blaine took Mia from her, carried her up the bank and lay her on the floor. Mia's face was cold and white; her dark hair flopped across it. Snakeskin came galloping up on her horse and in no time was at Mia's side. She started dropping a remedy onto Mia's lips and rubbing her arms and legs. Jack ran and sat next to Mia and immediately started doing CPR. It came back naturally to him, as if he did it all the time. He had never thought he would need to use the skills he had learned when his dad was ill. He pumped her chest and started breathing into her mouth. Snakeskin watched while reciting words under her breath. Mede started pecking at Mia's hands as if to wake her and Stan kept barking, "Mia, Mia." Suddenly, Mia arched her back and started coughing, water spluttering out of her mouth. Jack gasped for breath, as if he was breathing for her. Mia then took a breath and her eyes flickered open. Jack stared at her. Mia took a few big, heavy breaths, coughing a lot, then her breathing settled a little. Jack gasped, the relief flooding through him, and he grabbed Mia and hugged her hard, but his body started shaking and his teeth chattering.

"Mia, Mia, are you OK?" he asked urgently.

Mia mumbled into his shoulder, but he couldn't make out the words.

"We must get her warm," said Snakeskin, pulling clothes from her bag.

Aster passed over her heavy outer top. Blaine had a blanket on his horse, and they wrapped Mia in it while Snakeskin dropped some more liquid onto her lips and rubbed a salve into Mia's forehead.

All around them, the clouds were building into layers

of monster-like shapes, getting darker and thicker with every passing minute. The sun disappeared behind them, and the air felt electric; the hairs on Jack's arms stood on end. Blaine turned to Snakeskin. "The storm is getting closer. We must get to the gathering camp now – it is prepared. We need to get Mia onto a horse – maybe she can ride with you, Snakeskin, she needs someone to hold her," he said.

They lifted Mia carefully up onto Flint, in front of Snakeskin. Ayah perched on Snakeskin's shoulder, watching Mia intently.

"Do you think the wolves can make it?" asked Snakeskin, deep concern in her voice. The pack were still lying together by the riverbank. Wolf was now with them; her head was laid across another pack member, her eyes shut.

"We will walk with them," said Aster. "When you get to camp, ask Hal to come and meet us. He could bring some of the others; maybe they can help to carry the cubs."

A little further along the bank, Mist was standing, looking forlorn, a look of failure. Blaine called her over.

"Mist, would you be able to carry Jack? None of this was your fault – you must know that you did all you could. The world is not normal right now," he said as he rubbed her neck. Mist bowed her head.

"I would like to carry Jack if he will let me," Mist said quietly.

"Of course. It was not your fault – of course I want to ride with you. Stan can sit with me," said Jack.

"I'm thankful we made it this far, but we must get you all warm and rested," said Snakeskin. "I fear that is the last we will see of the sun now for some time. We need to get to the camp." And she rode forward.

Jack could see Mia was looking unresponsive and floppy in front of Snakeskin. He felt his fear rise up again. Snakeskin was singing and murmuring words in Mia's ear as they rode along.

"Snakeskin, what about the healing crystal we used on Stan? I have it here," called Jack.

"Thank you," said Snakeskin. "Yes, that will help."

Jack leaned forward and passed the crystal to Snakeskin; she tucked it into Mia's closed fist. The wind bit into Jack's wet T-shirt; he felt bitterly cold. He was glad of Stan's body warmth; he held his dog close. Up ahead, he could see Mede struggling to fly in the wind. Jack called out and Mede flew down.

"May I?" asked Mede as he landed on Jack's shoulder.

"Of course." Jack nodded.

Blaine rode around among them, handing out some of the hard acorn bread. It was damp and soggy from the river, but it was food all the same. Jack ate in exhausted silence. Trailing behind them was the wolf pack, with Aster doing her best to carry the youngest cubs. Wolf did not have her usual poise or strength and was walking with her tail between her legs and her head low.

They rode on, entering the immense forest of mesmerising white trees. Sounds of voices and drums travelled on the wind.

"What's that?" Jack asked.

"We are nearing the camp and the Great Fire Gathering," said Snakeskin. "There will be many people and creatures there now. As Aster told you, they have come from far and wide."

Jack could smell wood smoke and food cooking. His tummy rumbled. A sudden lightning strike lit up the forest around them; the sheer enormity of it was breathtaking and enchanting. The trees stood tall, straight and majestic, with exquisite white trunks, like giant church pillars. But they had round black marks on the trunks that seemed to stare out at them; Jack felt like he was being watched by thousands of eyes. Snakeskin turned in her saddle to face Jack. He gasped seeing Lela's eyes as they were burning molten white, a reflection from the lightning-bright trees.

Lela spoke, her slow, song-like voice ringing out clearly.

"Jack, you need to be prepared to meet Eye, the Great Elder. He is known in your time as the Pando. He has lived on this earth for tens of thousands of years and carries the ancient knowledge. He will be with you through this."

What or who was that ancient, that mystical? Jack's mind started racing. Wasn't Taxus the oldest tree in the wood? Maybe not in this land. Jack's heart pounded, excited and fearful. Lela turned to look at him, as if she could hear his heart. Her eyes seemed to flash between red and white and her body shimmered again, glowing bigger than her natural form.

"Jack, do not fear. Legend says that his eyes watch

humankind to ensure they are respectful. We know you are respectful. You have nothing to fear," she said gently.

Jack nodded to Lela, but was not sure he felt any less fearful. A loud crack of thunder trembled the forest. Jack shuddered. Whatever was about to happen started to feel very big.

Chapter 13

They rounded a bend and the forest opened into a giant glade. In the clearing was a vast camp, with a huge fire burning in the middle, and around the edge were shelters of all shapes and sizes. The elegant, white trees framed the whole scene.

People from all different clans and cultures were busy around the camp. Their dress, skin colour and hair all different to each other. It looked rather like a huge festival. As they rode through the camp, people stopped, animals turned, and he felt many eyes watching them. Some said 'hello' or '*welcome*'; others just looked or smiled.

There were also many different animals: at one glance Jack could see bison, horses, wild cats, beavers, otters, deer, wolves, foxes, squirrels, rabbits. A pair of golden eagles were sitting in the branches of one of the tallest aspen trees and other birds of all sorts were perched or flying around. He could also see insects, bees, butterflies and moths, all being buffeted by the wind. The middle of the circle stood empty, except for the enormous fire, and those tending it. The circle felt special somehow, like it was kept clear for a reason. They stopped near the fire and the feeling of warmth wrapped around Jack. He stumbled as he dismounted, his legs and back stiff. Remembering, he quickly turned to Mist and rubbed her neck, whispering, "Thank you," into her ear.

"You are welcome, Jack. We are all thankful you are here and of course Mia and Stan too," she said, then she nodded her head and turned and walked to join the rest of the herd.

A young man walked over and gave Jack a blanket. He wrapped it around his shoulders, feeling relief flood through him. He watched as Mia was lifted down from Snakeskin's horse and laid on a pile of blankets by the fire. Snakeskin whispered in the horse's ear, and it trotted off to join the herd, who were now rolling and grazing nearby. Jack watched for a moment as Mist, Rock and Flint all nuzzled each other and gently chewed each other's necks – it looked very loving.

As Jack was walking over towards Mia, he heard a cheer from across the camp. Turning, he saw Aster and a group of young people entering with the wolves. Wolf was leading but she was limping and looked weak and tired. People ran to them with food. It was then that Jack realised that Sylvie was standing to one side watching Aster arrive, she looked smaller somehow and her face was pale. Jack watched as Aster put the wolf cubs down, ran to Sylvie and flung her arms around her friend. Jack wondered what had changed since they last saw her, and if she really could no longer hear the trees and animals. He turned away and walked over to Mia, just as she sat up.

"Oh, Mia, are you OK?" he asked.

"That was just the worst thing. Oh, Jack, Wolf saved me, you know. She saw me and came after me." Her words were hurried but weak. "She left the pack and swam with me, and she kept grabbing at me and pulling me up, holding onto my clothes with her mouth. Then I felt a branch wrap around me or something, but I don't remember what happened after that, until you were doing something that felt like CPR," said Mia.

"It was CPR," said Jack, "and it was Alder's branch that caught you."

"How do you know CPR?" said Mia, with something that sounded like her old ridicule. With everything that had gone on, Jack had to smile at the fact that Mia seemed more surprised at such a practical thing like CPR, than by a wolf trying to save her. Jack was glad that she still had her feisty tone; he hoped it meant she was OK.

"Shhhh," said Snakeskin. "Mia, you must rest – you will have time to chat later." Jack looked up and saw Wolf padding over towards them; she bowed and touched her nose to Mia. Mia laid her hand on Wolf's neck and started quietly crying.

"Thank you, thank you," Mia said softly through her tears.

Wolf curled up by Mia and she laid on Wolf's neck, her

head buried in her fur, life and warmth flowing back into their bodies.

Snakeskin moved away from them and took her bundle of sticks some distance from the fire. Then, by the light of the fire, she walked around the circle, and at regular intervals stopped to push a stick into the ground. Blaine and Aster's brother Hal followed her, then Aster, hand in hand with Sylvie, joined them. Each time Snakeskin pushed a stick into the ground, she paused and quietly muttered some words. Finally, there was a circle of nine sticks surrounding the Great Fire. Snakeskin stood tall and called out, "Come, Jack, Mia, I need you. Jack, stand here," she said, pointing to two of the sticks. With the blanket still around his shoulders, Jack helped Mia to stand and walk to the nearest stick, and then he went to the next one. Wolf went and sat at Mia's feet, and Stan sat with Jack.

The group stood around the circle and Snakeskin let out a mighty cry, haunting and defiant. The ground started shaking and Jack saw a light come up through the ground, through the sticks. Suddenly, the sticks grew and pulsed with energy. He couldn't believe his eyes: where all the sticks had been placed, the magnificent Tree Council had appeared. Tears welled in his eyes. There was something so reassuring about seeing the mighty trees, the trees he knew from his home, standing in a circle, in this strange place, in this strange time. He flung his arms around Feya's strong trunk, feeling utter relief. Mia was now sitting with Ogham the Oak, Aster with Dancer the Ash, Blaine with

Taxus the Yew and Snakeskin with Alder the Protector. He looked around the circle and could see Gebo the Birch, the old, gnarled hawthorn and the hornbeam, all from the Tree Council, and joining them was also a mighty cedar tree. Jack let out a huge sigh, utterly speechless. Stan came over and snuffled Jack's hand.

"You OK?" Stan asked.

Jack nodded, then sat at the roots of Feya and cuddled Stan, just like he had that first day in the woods. Feya spoke: "Jack, you have done so well; the journey has been hard."

"Feya, I am so glad to see you," said Jack as he laid his hand on the smooth, grey bark, so familiar and gentle.

"We know it has been tough," said Feya, "but we do need to ask more of you. We will continue to do all we can to support and protect you, but The Forgetting's pain is beyond bounds now and the storm is close; you need to rest tonight," she said softly. "Ogham will say the same to Mia."

He looked over and saw Mia was now curled up at the foot of Ogham. Wolf was lying with her, a blanket wrapped around them. Feya spoke again. "Jack, lie down with me and listen to all the sounds, concentrate only on the sounds, for Eye has a message for you. Shut your eyes."

Jack did as he was asked, and in no time, he felt as if he was being carried into the enormous white trees. There was deep silence, nothing stirred, he couldn't even hear the footsteps of whoever was carrying him; the only thing he could hear was something like a deep heartbeat.

It was as if he were watching himself in a dream, real but not real: He was carried into a clearing deep in the forest, surrounded by the majestic white trunks, all reaching up to the sky above him. Then, he was lain down, and Mia was lain next to him.

"Jack… Jack… Jack." A deep, slow voice was calling him. "I have waited for you. Over the years, we have called out through the network, called and called for someone from your time to listen. Your father heard, Jack, but he was taken from us too soon. Then, the Elders, the Tree Council from your time, alerted me; they saw something special in you – you were still connected to the plants. Jack, I am Eye, the Great Elder, known also as the Pando; I am an aspen, Jack, and what might surprise you to know is that this whole forest is me. I am one being, with one root. I have stood on this land for tens of thousands of sun years; I am one of the oldest beings that exists. I have been here since some of the first peoples walked this land. I have watched humans and the world change, and I have survived some very extreme happenings, but now, in your time, too much is being destroyed and The Forgetting is now intent on destruction, her pain too great. The lifeblood is faltering, and my spirit weakens." Eye paused for a moment. "The storm of extinction is nearly upon us, but you are the hope, you, and Mia. Your arrival gives us a chance. You have shown such bravery on your journey. You are the best chance we have."

Jack lay listening, aware of eyes watching him from the trunks all around him. He felt as if the 'eyes' were looking right inside of him. Suddenly, he started getting flashes of his past again, flashes of him happy in the woods with his dad, flashes of his dad talking to the trees, flashes of Tom goading him and everyone laughing, but Eye spoke again, stopping the images and bringing his mind back to the white trunks surrounding him.

"I know you were told too often that you were not normal, but it is just because people have forgotten so much. The very thing that maybe made you feel as if you did not fit in, is the very reason why we need you." There was a pause. Jack lay in the peaceful silence of the forest.

"Jack, under you are my roots – they travel for miles through the earth; do not forget that. If you need me, I am here, even if it is not obvious. We will come together, supporting each other, a web to help our earth's protector to transform The Forgetting into remembering to help the earth find life and balance again. Always through death there can be new life. We believe in you. Keep awake; keep alert; and follow your heart."

With that, the voice stopped, and Jack half opened his eyes to find he was lying curled at Feya's roots, still wrapped in the warm blanket. He looked up and could see Mia asleep by Ogham. He rested his head back down and Stan curled up tighter against him.

Chapter 14

A loud drumming woke Jack and the urgency and tone of it vibrated through his belly; it was clear something had changed. The quiet softness of the night had been replaced by a blanket of peculiar red light, almost like an eclipse, it was not like anything he had ever seen. He got up and looked all around; Stan followed him. Everything felt strange, there was an eerie unsettling stillness and silence.

Jack surveyed the white forest surrounding them, the dream and the immense being of Eye filling his thoughts. He looked around the Tree Council circle, standing tall around the fire. He was so glad of their presence, their wisdom, their friendship. A group of beavers were rolling logs towards the fire and people were piling them up high. The fire was huge, deep orange flames leaping skywards. Snakeskin and a group of women were busy preparing a large rock that was just in front of the circle of the Tree Council, adorning it with flowers and leaves. Snakeskin looked solemn and did not speak to anyone. Jack watched for a moment, until Stan nudged at him with his nose. He turned to see Aster wake Mia.

"Let's go over to them," said Stan.

"Yes," said Jack, setting off towards them, the blanket still draped around his shoulders, keeping some sense of the night's peace wrapped around him. Mia was sitting with Wolf, her arm resting on Wolf's back.

"Mia, are you OK?" asked Jack.

"Yes, surprisingly OK," she said. "It's weird, I really feel alright, but I had this strange dream last night, or something like a dream. I was taken to meet a tree called Eye, the Great Elder. I'm not really sure how, but I was lying there, and he started talking to me and telling me that you and I are the one chance to right things here and that he or it is the whole of this white forest, and it's all one being."

"So did I!" said Jack. "And he talked about today being really important, and to remember the roots and the strength of the trees and about how what we change now will help change the future and our world," said Jack, a quizzical look on his face. They were quiet for a moment, both seeming lost in their thoughts.

"But I also saw all these images from my past: I saw me with my dad and the trees, but then…" Jack paused for a moment, as if unsure whether he should go on. Mia looked at him. "…Then, I saw you and Tom and other people bullying me."

"Oh," Mia said. There was a moment of silence between them.

"I'm sorry, Jack, I wish, I..." She stumbled over her words. "I saw images too. Of Tom being mean and teasing me, and my dad blaming me for everything, and I saw us doing stupid stuff to you. I'm so sorry," she mumbled.

"Stupid isn't exactly the word I would use," he said, "but I get it now."

They were interrupted by Aster running over. "Jack, Mia, we need to hurry now – the storm is close. Lela says we have little time, but you must eat for strength." Aster paused, realising too late that she had interrupted something. She stood, a little awkwardly, holding the bowls of food.

"Thank you," Jack said, trying to raise a smile as he reached for the bowls. They ate what they could of the warm, nutty porridge, but nerves made it hard to swallow. Jack looked up at Aster. "Aster, um, I saw you with Sylvie – is she OK?" he asked.

Aster looked at the ground for a moment. "She's OK," she said quietly. "She does not hear the trees anymore, and is sad, but she is trying to hold on."

"Oh, I am sorry," said Jack.

"We have to help her, Jack," said Aster softly and turned back to the fire. Jack silently watched her walk away, back to Sylvie who was standing quietly by the fire. He shoved his hands in his pockets, feeling their sorrow. His fingers touched his wolf carving in his pocket – he pulled it out and held it tight in his palm, but as he did, another piece of wood fell out of his pocket. He picked it up and looked at it.

"Mia, look, it's the ash wood, remember, it wards off bad energy. Have you got yours?"

Mia felt around and pulled out the hard piece of bark. "Do you really think we can make a difference?" she asked.

"We have to hope so," said Jack.

Aster reappeared, holding two beautiful dark wooden staffs, the wood rubbed to a shine. "Snakeskin says you must carry these. They are made from blackthorn. They carry special powers. The force of cleansing and the strength to complete a task," she said, passing them one each.

Mia held hers a little cautiously, while Jack turned his in his hand – it felt good, strong. He heard the echo of his dad's voice again. "*The trees are more special than you know, Jack.*"

A sudden sharp crack of thunder made them all jump. Stan sprung off the ground four feet at once. They all burst out laughing, but the butterflies in Jack's belly didn't stop. A sudden intense flash of lightning lit up the white forest all around them. The air tingled. Huge drops of rain started falling with heavy, loud thuds, leaving tiny craters in the dust. A deep, earthy, musty smell filled the air. Aster looked towards her mum, fear now clear in her face. Jack flinched, as suddenly the world started to waver again; it was as if there was a mirage in front of the world he was in, where fires were raging, trees burning, everything crashing down. Then it shuddered and shifted back to the gathering camp. Jack looked around. Fear surged through him, but then the powerful collective voice of the Tree Council echoed around the camp.

"Hold firm – it is time! All those gathered, you know what to do. Form into circles around the fire. Everyone must touch. Every circle counts. Remember we are a web!"

"Quick! We must get into the circle. Mia, grab your staff!" Aster shouted as she seized Sylvie's hand and ran towards Snakeskin. Jack and Mia rushed after them with Stan scurrying at their heels.

"Mia, Jack, Aster, Hal, you must make the first circle with the Tree Council. Jack and Mia, you will stand either side of me," called Snakeskin, over the oncoming breaking storm. "Don't forget, together, we have the strength and the power of remembering."

People and animals were gathering around the fire in giant circles.

"Together, we have the strength. The fire of transformation is before us," echoed the collective voice of the Tree Council.

The wind was getting stronger by the second, swirling in eddies around them. The dust and leaves blew in their faces. Jack blinked, his eyes smarting. Thunder cracks bellowed overhead, shaking the land under their feet. The trunks of Eye were swaying, branches rattling, and the giant forest seemed to glow, its eyes watching, ready. The beavers and fire keepers were piling the fire high with dead wood from the forest and, despite the rain, the flames leapt high into the air. The drumming was getting louder and louder, then all around them a deep humming started – it came from the white forest, from Eye the Great Elder, and reverberated through Jack's whole body. There was no turning back.

Chapter 15

The Tree Council stood tall and majestic in the first circle around the fire, their huge trunks magnificent, their roots making a glowing web underfoot. Snakeskin stood by the large rock between Ogham the Oak and Taxus the Yew, where she and the group of women had prepared the alter of flowers and crystals. Jack was on one side of her, and Mia on the other. Stan was sitting at Jack's feet and Wolf was standing next to Mia. Beside them stood Aster, Sylvie and Hal. In between the other Tree Council trees stood Blaine, and many different Clan Elders, both human and animal. Beavers, foxes, deer, otters, bison, Blaine's mighty horse Rock, and in the branches of the trees sat Owl, Mede, Ayah and the pair of eagles, all collectively making a circle with the Tree Council. Everyone and everything else made larger and large circles behind them, like tree rings themselves. People stood holding hands, holding animals, touching trees, defiant. Eye called out, "We are a web; everyone is connected. Every one of us counts."

Snakeskin's gaze was fixed ahead of her, looking deep into the Pando Forest, to Eye the Great Elder. She turned and looked around the circles, her face tense and sad, raw with emotion. She slowly uncurled Lela the snake from around her neck, who slithered down her arm and onto the large rock in front of her. Snakeskin stroked her hand along the snake's body, and Jack saw the shimmering again. It was as if her body went beyond her skin, her being greater than the skin.

Lela spoke calmly, her voice carrying over the storm, with a strength far beyond her size: "We are all here for this, the most important event of our lives, and of all time, The Remembering ceremony. We have prepared long and hard for this moment, a moment that could change everything, stop The Forgetting and bring balance back to the world. My life's work is done."

Snakeskin stood strong and composed, but the tears were welling in her eyes as Lela spoke.

"Eye, you have taught me well and when I accepted this task, I knew that one day if our plan worked, it would come to this. Snakeskin, you have been a true friend and student. Together we have travelled the network, far and wide, to prepare, and you have done all you can now to help me. I accept this, my destiny, with honour and hope." Lela's voice was full of love. She raised her head to Snakeskin and looked her in the eyes.

Snakeskin, with tears streaming down her face, removed a sharp crystal knife from inside the beautiful bead pouch that hung around her neck. The snake laid herself down on the rock, but Snakeskin's hands trembled with the task before her. Jack stood watching, unblinking. A sense of foreboding filled the air, and silent tears ran down Aster's cheeks. It felt like even the wind quietened for a moment.

"It is time," said Lela. "Peace be with you all. I release to bring balance, and remembering," she hissed with a calm, clear voice.

Snakeskin slowly ran her hand down the snake's back, rolled Lela over, and then slowly sliced along the snake's soft underbelly. As she did, there was a loud hiss, like water escaping from a hydrant. There was a gasp around the circle and Jack felt sick as he watched, but out of the snake a light flowed, and out of the light a translucent shape formed. It was like an iridescent light prism, glinting like sunlight on water as it moved, different colours bouncing all around the circle. Jack realised that this was the shimmer he had seen around Lela. He watched, captivated. Slowly, the shape took more form: it was like a giant snake, but with a head a bit like a horse's, and with immense gossamer wings. Jack gasped – it was exquisite, but unlike anything he had ever seen or even read about; it was more beautiful and more magical, but not quite there, a mirage, ghostly.

The light from the fire bounced off the creature, so that even in the red darkness of the storm, it was as if the fire was spiralling in the sky. The creature started to make a sound, a deep sound, like a whale song but deeper, rumbling through the air. Snakeskin stood by the rock, grief-stricken but strong and upright; she looked majestic.

Then Eye's voice rang out, loud and deep. "Lela has given her form to release the only thing left that can help us. Efil, we are honoured by your presence."

Aster and Hal were crying and holding hands next to Jack, looking up at the beast above them. Snakeskin picked up Lela's' body, sprinkled something onto it, then carefully wrapped it in a beautiful cloth and placed it in her bag. The wind started to pick up again.

"Welcome, Efil," echoed the Tree Council trees.

The welcome call then grew on the wind, rippling around the circles, rumbling around the crowd and animals. Eye's voice bellowed through the forest and across the land, as if it came from under their feet.

"Efil is Earth's Protector!" Eye called out. "She is as ancient as the land itself, carrying the knowledge from across time. She is life force and memory, the true balance to destruction. We know The Forgetting is seeking her out, wanting to draw her, us all, into the ancient gloom. We had to keep her safe and hidden to maintain her strength. Lela has made the ultimate sacrifice, carrying and protecting Efil, while we prepared for this ceremony to restore the earth's equilibrium and help humans to remember. Lela and Snakeskin have protected her and carried her in silence. Snakeskin, your service and loyalty to Efil and the earth are unequalled."

The huge crowd were silent and still, standing in their circles, watching. Eye's many great trunks were glowing white, and the forest felt alive and powerful. But the calm was subsiding, the wind growing stronger and grumbling thunder rolling back around. Eye spoke louder. "Jack and Mia, your role becomes clear; your task is not a small one. Efil needs to find her full form through all of us, so she has the power to transform The Forgetting. We are all going to need to combine our energy. But to have people from your time, from the real dying time, is crucial. Your strength and focus are of utmost importance, so the healing can carry across time."

The sky lit up with a burst of lightning and Eye shuddered. "Remember to stay connected! Every one of us counts; everyone here is needed. Do not break the circle. The Root Network is flowing beneath us, connecting us all here and across time. Jack and Mia, Efil needs to find form through you. Trust and be brave," Eye called out with force.

As the words were spoken, everything changed. The wind grew into a violent whirling vortex and thunder cracked overhead. Giant forks of lightning struck the ground, burning into the earth, and where they hit, fractures started appearing all around them, creating gaping holes just outside of the circle. A dark, silvery, mist-like form started to creep out of the holes, its fingers reaching, searching. People started to run and scatter.

"*Stop!*" called Ogham.

"*Hold your circles!*" called Eye. "We must stand firm. Do *not* run. Our sacred circle is strong – we can hold it back, but only together." Eye's voice was fierce and commanding.

Efil lifted her head, bent low and breathed long and hard onto the fire. The flames blazed and burned with greater intensity, leaping up into the darkening sky.

"Jack, Mia, we need you now. Give Efil your strength. You need to touch her, so the energy flows from all of us through you," Snakeskin called suddenly.

Jack stretched up to touch Efil, but she was out of reach.

"Use your staffs!" Snakeskin commanded.

Jack held his blackthorn staff and reached up, so that it touched the bouncing light, and instantly the creature started to become less transparent, more opaque.

"Mia, touch her too," Jack yelled, "use your staff gently."

Mia reached up with her staff, and where she touched the light, the creature's form settled further. Then Efil arched, vibrated and formed into a solid shape. She was a deep iridescent green, shimmering like the feathers on a drake's neck. Jack gulped at her sheer beauty and size. Efil turned, her red eyes full of power. It was the same fire-like look Jack had seen in Lela's eyes.

The wind was swirling in mini tornados, buffeting and pummelling them relentlessly. The dark shadow form was seeping along the ground, through the mighty Pando forest of Eye the Elder. Huge drops of hail started to fall, burning Jack's face; he blinked hard. The hail made a layer of what looked like white marbles on the ground. Efil breathed into the Great Fire, and with each breath, it seemed to burn with a greater power and intensity.

People were chanting, animals howling, barking, screeching, baying.

"Now what?" called Jack.

"Now we stop our forgetting and halt the storm it brings. We help people remember, remember they have a choice," called Efil. Her voice was like music: clear, powerful and strong enough to cut through the wind.

"What does that mean?" shouted Mia, looking over at Jack.

"I don't know!" shouted Jack.

From the great forest around them, from the Great Elder, Eye, came a cry. "It means we combine our energy. It means we do everything we can to banish the destruction that has caused this," he bellowed. "We suck it from the earth and then The Remembering, the rebalancing, can start. Focus all your energy into Efil; give her the power to fight the storm; and in your hearts and minds, hold the word 'remembering'. Banish the destruction; banish The Forgetting from our world. Focus on balance and the energy of the Root Network connecting us across time, pushing out the ancient fault line in our earth. It is time for The Remembering." The powerful words of Eye reverberated through the storm, as if bouncing off walls; they echoed around them: 'balance' and 'remembering', repeating again and again.

The words and sounds of all the people and creatures and trees in the many rings around the fire built from a hum to a cacophony. Efil's mighty breath blew on the fire; it burned with a vivid white, dazzling light. The fire keepers were still feeding the flames with old, dead, dried wood. The trees were chanting loud and clear. The forest that was Eye, the hundreds of acres of one voice, chanted: "*Remember.*"

Jack started to feel his legs going numb, his body faltering.

"Mia!" he shouted, but as he did, he fell to the floor, the energy with Efil broken.

Stan ran over to him and started licking his face. Mia looked, but did not move, she determinedly kept her staff in contact with the great beast. Then, suddenly, she screamed out.

"I can't hold on! Efil, Taxus, Ogham, help! Jack, I'm..." But her words faltered, and she too fell to the floor. Wolf ran to Mia and licked her forehead and hands to rouse her. Above them, Efil flickered and started to lose form.

A violent cracking sound signalled the opening of a huge fracture that cut through the forest of Eye, stopping just at the edge of the sacred circle. The silver-grey molten shadow form of The Forgetting started to rise, coiling around the structures on the edge of the circle, but it could not enter the circle, the force of the gathering holding it back. It kept growing in size, reaching up and around, its mercury-like form becoming stronger, the silver darker.

Eye let out a piercing wail and started quaking. Fire started to burn some of the trunks of the mighty forest. The ground shuddered. Snakeskin darted to Jack and Mia and put a drop from her pouch onto each of their lips.

"It is the tonic gift from Hornbeam. It will relieve you of your exhaustion," she said. "We have to try again! Do not give up! Draw on all the reserves you have!"

Blaine broke from the circle and appeared at their side. He whistled, and Mist and his horse Rock came cantering over. Blaine lifted Jack onto Rock's back, and Mia onto Mist's. "They need more energy. They are too small and do not have enough power on their own. Come quickly," he called to Aster and Sylvie. "We need you. Come, jump behind each of them and hold them steady – your combined energy is what is needed. Sylvie, this too will change your future – you need to find your strength." Blaine's voice was urgent but clear.

Jack had Sylvie sitting behind him and Mia had Aster. They handed them their staffs.

"You need to make contact again," said Blaine.

Stan sat next to Jack's horse, watching him.

"Jack, I am here," called Stan. "Remember, I am here. Your dad would be so proud of you, Jack!"

Jack sat up. This had to work – he wanted a world where he could talk to his dog, where he could consider trees as friends without being called weird or being bullied, and where the continual and dreadful destruction of the forests would be brought to a stop. And he wanted a world in which Sylvie was OK. Stan was sitting bolt upright, focused on the young people, his eyes full of pride and concentration. The sky above them opened to reveal deeper, angrier-looking dark, red clouds, like a raging burning star above them. The wind howled with ferocious intensity and thunder boomed every few seconds.

Ogham spoke loud above the storm. "Tree Council, focus your energy on Mia and Jack. They need our life force. Everyone else, do not stop remembering; keep connection between man and plant, man and animal, man and the land. Banish the ancient void. Do *not* stop," he called with his booming voice.

At that, Dancer the Ash, with a mighty shudder, moved the whole of her crown towards Efil, her energy flowing into the creature and to Jack and Mia. Jack suddenly felt his strength grow; he saw the roots all around him glowing and the energy flowing up into him. His arms felt like branches reaching up to Efil. He thought of the trees in his time, the ones that needed saving, and the animals, and felt a voice rise within him. He shouted with all his might, "Dad, we will stop The Forgetting!"

In the light from the fire, he saw his dad pick him up onto his shoulders like he did when he was young. He felt strong and alive and lifted his staff to touch Efil's wing. Mia did the same, the effort clear in her face. Sylvie and Aster supported both their arms, the energy streaming from their small bodies through into Efil. Efil's shape grew strong again, her wings now transforming into wings of pure fire.

A loud crash and a sharp fork of lightning hit at that moment. It struck Ogham, and a huge branch split from his trunk. His war cry scream reverberated around the circle, and there was a collective gasp.

After a moment he called, "I am still here! We must continue. Take my branch to the fire." The pain was evident in his voice, but so was his determination. He was an oak, the tree of the gods, and he drew on his own deep and ancient power.

As they added the branch to the fire, the fire leapt higher, and Efil filled with flames that spread all through her full form. She became a flying fire creature. She opened her great flaming mouth, and as the storm raged, she started to suck the dark, molten energy of The Forgetting out of the earth. Jack kept his focus but watched in amazement as the silvery, mercury-like form started to flow up from the earth and into Efil's mouth. Her body started to grow and shimmer. There was a bleak, deep gurgle which became a scream from deep within the battling force. The dark, silver energy was battling with her fire – they looked like a wild storm glass.

She writhed and writhed, but silvery, arm-like tentacles stretched out to grab at people in the circle. They reached for Jack and Mia, but Efil turned and spun, so the being was flung sideways and not able to take hold.

Tears of effort were streaming down Jack and Mia's cheeks and the strain showed too on Aster and Sylvie's faces. The horses, miraculously, stood stock still.

Then Efil started to spin and spin, faster and faster. Swirling, with her mouth open. As she whirled, the ancient being – the layers of sadness, of destruction and the storm – started to be drawn into her mouth; The Forgetting was being pulled from out of the ground. Its long 'fingers' of grey energy clung onto the earth, but as Efil spun faster and faster, it started losing its grip and spinning with her. Jack felt his own body shudder and saw Mia shaking, as if something was being pulled from them too. The earth around them, the roots, the trees were all shuddering, branches rattling.

Then the mass of the ancient shadow, the water, the rain, the hail, the wind, the thunder, the mighty clouds and the dark vapour all started rotating like a whirlwind down into the mouth of Efil, and as it did, it was as if her body followed it and started to fall in on itself. A dark swirling, screaming, battling, clashing mass.

There was an almighty cracking noise and flash of silver light, and the complete black mass of energy fell in on itself and disappeared into the fire.

Everything stopped. The fires vanished; the fissures in the earth stopped spitting. The silver curling mercury substance had gone. The rain stopped. The wind stopped. Efil had gone. There was a sudden and complete silence.

Jack and Mia fell forward onto the necks of their horses and Aster and Sylvie sat slumped holding on behind them. The horses kept their vigil and didn't move, but the sweat drenched their necks. Everyone stood for a moment, watching, waiting, as if they were holding their breath. There was just the sound of water dripping from branches, pure rain, not Dark Rain. Blaine rushed over, and the other Clan Elders followed. They gently lifted the children down and laid them at the foot of Feya and Ogham, wrapping them in blankets. Snakeskin stood silently watching. Slowly, quietly, people started to attend to the injured around them, both people and animals alike. Some stood hugging, holding hands, in disbelief, relief and sheer exhaustion.

The red light had gone and before long, the clouds overhead parted enough for evening sunlight to glint off the wet trees. Jack sat quietly with Mia, wrapped in the coloured blankets, Stan, and Wolf beside them, too exhausted to speak. As Jack watched, he felt strange; it was as if people were almost moving in slow motion around him. He reached out his hand to touch Feya's familiar smooth bark, and he held his hand there for a moment, trying to grasp what had just happened.

Aster walked to Sylvie, and they stood holding each other, then slowly walked to join Mia and Jack. In shock, they all gazed at the broken and burned trees within the forest of Eye, the mighty Pando. All that was left of the fire and of Efil were some grey, smouldering embers. The smell of ash and smoke filled the air.

"Jack, you should be truly proud. All of you should be," said Feya quietly.

They looked at each other and smiled, not yet able to comprehend and too tired to talk.

Jack watched as Snakeskin walked to the remains of the fire, with Ayah perched on one shoulder and Mede on the other. The three surveyed the ashes, and suddenly Mede swooped down, just as he had when he'd seen the droplet in Stan's cut. He flew into the embers and pulled out a tiny ball, the size of a large marble. Mede held it in his beak and flew back to Snakeskin. Jack could see that inside the ball it swirled like it was full of fire and light; it was alive in some way. Mede dropped the ball into Snakeskin's hands; she held it momentarily to her heart, then lifted it up and studied it. Rainbow light bounced around the circle, like the light from a prism. Snakeskin smiled. Eye's booming voice filled the space. "Snakeskin, you hold the life force of Efil, protected and safe. The pain of The Forgetting has been drawn out of the earth. Our Root Network will be safe, for now."

Everyone erupted in a giant cheer and Stan started barking and bouncing around.

The kids hugged each other and cheered. Jack bent down to hug Stan, who licked his face frantically. "Yuk," he said, laughing.

"You mean I'm not allowed to lick you anymore, just because you can hear me talk?" asked Stan.

"Ha, ha," said Jack, tousling his dog's hair.

"Some things won't change, you know," said Stan. "I'm still a dog, I still sniff bottoms and I like eating your sandwiches."

They all laughed. Jack turned to Mia, and they hugged, a huge, profound hug, tears welling in both their eyes. Snakeskin walked over to them.

"Mede has found the fireball in the embers; it is the life force of Efil, sacred to us all," said Snakeskin. "She is alive, but has returned to her birthing egg, where she holds the soul of the earth safe again. They will need time to heal and become strong once more, to restore balance, and during that time, the changes will start to ripple through the rings of time. Jack and Mia, you have one last very important task," she said, pausing for a moment.

"You must carry her precious form to your time and there you must take her to the ocean and release her to the water, where she will rest and regain her strength, protected in our mighty oceans. While that happens, the healing energy and The Remembering will also be carried through the waters, to every community on earth in your time; be it by sea, rain, mist or river, the water will travel – there are no barriers. Water holds memory. Keep her safe – that is your last and most important task." Snakeskin's voice was calm and loving.

Jack sat quietly, contemplating the deep responsibility.

"Thank you," he said, "we will take care of Efil, as you say."

Snakeskin very carefully handed Jack the pouch with the fireball resting inside. He held it gently in his hand, feeling it with his fingers, marvelling at it and how much trust they were putting in them.

Then Eye's voice echoed out once more. "All who have congregated here, we hope this will bring back balance to the soul of the world across time and stop humans forgetting. Today, we must celebrate the beginning of The Remembering. Everyone here has played their part – without each and every one of you, we would not have had the strength, that is clear. Jack and Mia, you will go back to a different world, but as The Forgetting has prevailed for so long, it will take time for the change to emerge; it will ripple through the Rings of Time, like a pebble dropped in water – change will come. Once The Remembering starts to filter through and all people begin to hear the language of the nature around them, just imagine what a world you will live in. You will be pioneers in your time; you will help guide people and help them to see. Let the forests grow, Jack, Mia, fight for trees and the oceans. Be strong – carry in your heart the world you want to live in. Some people may be afraid and may fight against what they hear or what they feel, or they may worry about profit and business, so they will fight to keep it how it was. You must do all you can to tell the story of the trees and help people to remember. Do not forget, we will always be with you through the Root Network – do not allow The Forgetting to grow and to stalk this world again," said Eye.

When Eye finished, Jack ran and hugged Ogham as if he were his oldest and dearest friend. He reached up and touched the wound of the broken branch.

"I am alright," said Ogham, "it will heal, but remember, Jack, we are all stronger than we think, especially when we combine our might and knowledge. You do not need to worry." His voice was calm and resonant.

The reality of going home started to sink in, and Jack felt relief but also fear and dread; he couldn't really imagine going home now and what it would be like. Mia turned to him and met his gaze, as if sensing his apprehension, as if reading his mind.

"It will be different," she said.

Jack nodded. "Yeah, I know it will," he said.

"At least we'll both be grounded together!" she said, and they laughed at the strangeness of that thought.

But Jack knew he would miss his new friends; he would miss this beautiful world, brimming with wildlife and ancient trees.

"Snakeskin, do we have to walk all the way back through the Lock and the forest?" asked Jack, thinking back to the markers he left and the route he had tried to remember.

She smiled. "No, you do not have to walk – Taxus will be able to transport you. She is weaving that route now through the Root Network with Eye and the Council Elders, but first they all need to rest and regain their energy. You also need some food and rest to regain your own strength – your bodies are too weak to travel the network just now," she said. She looked exhausted, and spoke slowly, but the weight of sadness had lifted from her face.

"I'm sorry about Lela," Jack said quietly.

"Yes, so am I, but I know she has not gone. She will stay with me forever," she said, smiling a warm smile and putting her hand on her heart.

The fire keepers had rekindled the fire, and people were busy cooking and sitting in groups chatting.

"We might need to bring Tom one day, so he can see it all," said Mia, aware again of being separate from her twin for longer than ever before in her life. He would be very angry.

"That will be a good thing. You must hold out hope that he will understand; he certainly will come to understand in time," said Snakeskin. "So much has changed for you both; he will need a little time to adjust."

They all sat and ate and talked for a while. Jack, Mia and Aster were telling Sylvie and Hal about the journey, reliving all the events for a moment. Exhaustion kept coming in waves through Jack – he couldn't really believe what had just happened. Would it really make a difference? He hoped with all his heart it would.

"Soon, Taxus will carry you home," said Eye gently. "It has been most humbling to meet you, and you will always be held here in my eyes. Remember the network is always there, under you, to support you as you step back into your world."

"Thank you," said Jack. "I cannot imagine what it is like to live so long, you must have seen so much, I would like very much to come back and talk to you one day."

"Well, remember, Jack, I am in your time too, and I would very much like to share my stories with you. One day you might be able to visit me."

The sun had gone down behind the trees; the day was drawing to a close. Snakeskin gestured that it was time to go. Jack walked straight to Wolf and touched his nose to hers, and Wolf bowed down.

"Thank you," said Jack. "Thank you for saving Mia."

Mia then threw her arms around Wolf's neck and hugged and hugged her. Wolf licked Mia's hand. A single tear rolled down Mia's cheek. Wolf's eyes were full of kindness and gratitude. Jack felt like they had become Wolf's pack, her family, an unspoken bond joining them all. Aster and Sylvie walked over to them.

"We are going to miss you. Please come and visit," said Aster.

"We will definitely do that if we can," said Jack.

"You can come back to us via Feya or Taxus," said Snakeskin. "Come to the Council once the network has healed; you have earned that right. We can share information and it will be good to see you." Snakeskin held both their hands gently in hers. "Take care of Efil," she said.

Jack turned abruptly as he heard Stan say, "Are you OK, Sylvie?"

"Well, I can hear you, Stan," she said, smiling. She and Aster hugged and jumped up and down together.

"Wow, so it is changing already?"

"It is for me," said Sylvie, as she bent down to cuddle Stan. Jack smiled a broad smile.

Jack and Mia walked to Mist and Rock and whispered in their ears and rubbed their necks. Jack had discovered that he loved the smell of the horses; he buried his nose in Mist's fur and breathed in a deep breath, absorbing that sweet smell. She felt warm and comforting. He stood for some time, until Taxus called out, "We are ready – the Root Network is strong enough to take you home."

Jack's stomach twitched; he didn't really want to leave all these new friends. He walked around the tree circle, hugging each tree, running his fingers down their bark.

"I'll visit you in the woods really soon," he said.

From the branches above them, Mede cawed. Looking up, Jack and Mia called in unison, "Thank you, Mede."

The crow bowed his head to them. "I will see you again," he said.

Mia held out her arm and made her passionate call, and Ayah flew down and perched very gently on her arm, careful that her talons did not spike Mia's skin.

"Ayah, thank you, I wish you could come back with

us," said Mia, gently, reaching out and stroking the bird's powerful neck.

Ayah bowed her head. "I will see you again, Mia."

Snakeskin took their hands in hers. "It is time," she said. "You have been brave beyond words."

They ran and hugged Aster and Sylvie again, in a big group hug.

"I'm going to miss you," said Jack to Aster and Sylvie.

"Me too," said Mia.

Jack and Mia walked quietly to Taxus and stood inside the ancient tree, holding hands and holding onto Stan's collar.

"We could not have done this without you," said Taxus.

"Goodbye!" they shouted.

A mighty cheer and cacophony of animal noises signalled their send-off.

There was the familiar tug and the sensation of sliding and rolling through the earth and tree roots. Jack felt himself turn this way and that. Now he could clearly see pathways and tunnels through his half-open eyes, but it was over quickly, and with a jolt, Jack landed in a heap next to Mia and Stan, inside the trunk of the great yew. Jack looked up – it was dark and quiet, but the air felt warm. Stan nuzzled him with his wet nose. Jack reached out to touch Mia's hand.

"Are we really home? Did that really happen?" he whispered. As he did, he felt for Efil safe in his pocket. Touching her, he smiled. Suddenly, two large, green-yellow eyes appeared in front of them.

“Miaaaa,” came a thick, purring voice.

Jack and Mia both jumped. Stan let out a muffled yip.

“What is it?” said Jack, as warm fur brushed up against his arm.

“Conker!” said Mia in surprise.

“At last, you can hear me,” said Conker. “Listen! There are a lot of worried people out looking for you two; even Tom has been really upset. It is not going to be easy to explain, but Taxus and I have been hatching a plan, so you need to listen carefully.”

Acknowledgements

To Nick for being there always. Deep thanks to my editor, Sara Starbuck for your amazing guidance and wisdom. To my Allyu for your encouragement. To my family, my sisters, all my friends and friends' children who have read, encouraged, supported and reread. Extra thanks to Melissa Orrom Swan for your knowledge and advice and Jessica Kashdan-Brown for your notes early on and to Niki Jewett for your support and assistance. To London Lit Lab, especially Zoe Gilbert. To Ramona Ring for your perfect cover illustration. To Gemma Gawned for helping me believe. Thank you to the trees of the world, the guidance of all of nature and the paradise which is our planet earth.

There are some wonderful charities working with tree planting, regeneration, and rewilding.

A percentage of profit will be donated to:

The Tree Sisters. https://www.treesisters.org
Yorenka Tasorentsi Institute. https://yorenkatasorentsi.org
Trees for Cities: https://www.treesforcities.org

Website: www.dioneorrom.com

From the Author

My childhood home was a messy jumble of humans, animals, plants, art, and music. We lived on the edge of an ancient beech wood two miles from the nearest village. Important characters in my life were Chocolate the donkey, Fireball the pony, Bertie the chicken who lived in the kitchen when she was injured, Nibblet my pet rat that would hide behind my hair, and Emma and Pepe the goats who would come for walks to the woods. I loved following tracks and signs, catching a glimpse of the lives of wild creatures; or finding treasured fossils and crystals in the flint rocks scattered on the woodland floor, hinting of an ancient oceanic past.

A childhood that allowed me to listen to the stories of the world around me. When I found my shamanic path in my late 20's it confirmed to me how everything is interconnected and if we listen, the voices of trees, clouds, rocks, and the earth are clear to be heard, carrying such wisdom, reminding us we are not alone, everything is connected.

One great inspiration for me was Dr Zeus's powerful book The Lorax, a story that has stayed with me for life, it still makes me cry! Books are so powerful.

I heard the trees call for me to write this story, their story, their call for action and love.

I live on the edge of Bath in Somerset, with an array of animals, growing vegetables, foraging wild food and herbs and planting trees. My favourite way to spend a day is wandering the hills and woods with my beloved dog Obi (who is a Jedi!) listening to the whispers of the world around me.